One Hot
BASH

Other Books by Anna Durand

One Hot Chance (Hot Brits, Book One)
One Hot Roomie (Hot Brits, Book Two)
One Hot Crush (Hot Brits, Book Three)
The Dixon Brothers Trilogy (Hot Brits, Books 1-3)
One Hot Escape (Hot Brits, Book Four)
One Hot Rumor (Hot Brits, Book Five)
One Hot Christmas (Hot Brits, Book Six)
One Hot Scandal (Hot Brits, Book Seven)
One Hot Deal (Hot Brits, Book Eight)
One Hot Favor (Hot Brits, Book Nine)
Natural Obsession (Au Naturel Nights, Book One)
Natural Deception (Au Naturel Nights, Book Two)
Natural Passion (Au Naturel Trilogy, Book One)
Natural Impulse (Au Naturel Trilogy, Book Two)
Natural Satisfaction (Au Naturel Trilogy, Book Three)
Lachlan in a Kilt (The Ballachulish Trilogy, Book One)
Aidan in a Kilt (The Ballachulish Trilogy, Book Two)
Rory in a Kilt (The Ballachulish Trilogy, Book Three)
The American Wives Club (A Hot Brits/Hot Scots/Au Naturel Crossover)
Brit vs. Scot (A Hot Brits/Hot Scots/Au Naturel Crossover)
A Novel Secret (A Hot Brits/Hot Scots/Au Naturel Crossover) (
Dangerous in a Kilt (Hot Scots, Book One)
Wicked in a Kilt (Hot Scots, Book Two)
Scandalous in a Kilt (Hot Scots, Book Three)
The MacTaggart Brothers Trilogy (Hot Scots, Books 1-3)
Gift-Wrapped in a Kilt (Hot Scots, Book Four)
Notorious in a Kilt (Hot Scots, Book Five)
Insatiable in a Kilt (Hot Scots, Book Six)
Lethal in a Kilt (Hot Scots, Book Seven)
Irresistible in a Kilt (Hot Scots, Book Eight)
Devastating in a Kilt (Hot Scots, Book Nine)
Spellbound in a Kilt (Hot Scots, Book Ten)
Relentless in a Kilt (Hot Scots, Book Eleven)
Incendiary in a Kilt (Hot Scots, Book Twelve)
Wild in a Kilt (Hot Scots, Book Thirteen)
Unstoppable in a Kilt (Hot Scots, Book Fourteen)
The Notorious Dr. MacT (A Hot Scots Prequel)
The British Bastard (A Hot Scots Prequel)
Echo Power (Echo Power Trilogy, Book One)
Echo Dominion (Echo Power Trilogy, Book Two)
Echo Unbound (Echo Power Trilogy, Book Three)
The Mortal Falls (Undercover Elementals, Book One)
The Mortal Fires (Undercover Elementals, Book Two)
The Mortal Tempest (Undercover Elementals, Book Three)
The Janusite Trilogy (Undercover Elementals, Books 1-3)
Obsidian Hunger (Undercover Elementals, Book Four)
Unbidden Hunger (Undercover Elementals, Book Five)
The Thirteenth Fae (Undercover Elementals, Book Six)
Cyneric (Undercover Elementals, Book 7)

One Hot BASH

Hot Brits, Book Ten

ANNA DURAND

JACOBSVILLE BOOKS JB MARIETTA, OHIO`

ONE HOT BASH

Copyright © 2023 by Lisa A. Shiel
All rights reserved.

The characters and events in this book are fictional. No portion of this book may be copied, reproduced, or transmitted in any form or by any means, electronic or otherwise, including recording, photocopying, or inclusion in any information storage and retrieval system, without the express written permission of the publisher and author, except for brief excerpts quoted in published reviews.

ISBN: 978-1-958144-29-9 (paperback)
ISBN: 978-1-958144-30-5 (ebook)
ISBN: 978-1-958144-31-2 (audiobook)

Manufactured in the United States.

Jacobsville Books
www.JacobsvilleBooks.com

Publisher's Cataloging-in-Publication Data
provided by Five Rainbows Cataloging Services

Names: Durand, Anna.
Title: One hot bash / Anna Durand.
Description: Marietta, OH : Jacobsville Books, 2023. | Series: Hot Brits, bk. 10.
Identifiers: ISBN 978-1-958144-29-9 (paperback) | ISBN 978-1-958144-30-5 (ebook) | ISBN 978-1-958144-31-2 (audiobook)
Subjects: LCSH: Man-woman relationships--Fiction. | Butlers--Fiction. | Halloween--Fiction. | British--Fiction. | Americans--Fiction. | Romance fiction. | BISAC: FICTION / Romance / Contemporary. | FICTION / Romance / Romantic Comedy. | GSAFD: Love stories.
Classification: LCC PS3604.U724 O54 2023 (print) | LCC PS3604.U724 (ebook) | DDC 813/.6--dc23.

Prologue

Kendall
Four Months Ago

"Do you have a copy of that book? The sign in the window says you do, but I can't find it anywhere. You shouldn't announce it if you don't have the ruddy book in stock yet. Are you listening to me? I want the new Desiree Lachance romance. I don't think you're listening at all. Who is in charge of this shop? I insist upon speaking to the manager or whoever it is."

I pause in the midst of gift wrapping a travel guide for the gent who is leaning against the counter waiting for that. But he isn't the one speaking to me. No, it's the woman who pushed past him to get to me who won't stop talking. Her combative tone does nothing to ease my anxiety. Why on earth did I agree to manage Poppy Goodburn's bookshop whilst she's away in Scotland?

The woman smacks her palm down on the counter. "Wake up. Are you even old enough to work in a place that sells erotic romances? You're fifteen at the most."

I am far older than that. But my age is none of her concern.

Oh, good lord. How am I meant to survive the rest of today? The past four days had been hell. I think I actually saw the devil hiding in the shadows at the far corner of the shop, grinning with malevolent delight.

The woman is glowering at me intensely.

"L-let me find that book for you." Why am I stuttering? It's rubbish. "If you'll just give me a moment to finish wrapping up th-this—"

She puckers her lips and rolls her eyes. "Get on with it."

Miraculously, I manage to finish the gift-wrapping and drop the book into a paper sack, which I hand to the chap who's been waiting patiently.

He accepts the sack. "Thank you, son. You're doing a commendable job considering the amount of traffic in this shop."

"Ah…thank you?" I shouldn't have sounded uncertain, but my mind has melted, and I can't think straight anymore. Whilst the gent walks away, I turn to the woman. "Now, I will be happy to find that book for you."

She huffs. "About bloody time."

I whirl round to exit the area behind the counter, but I trip over a pile of books that had fallen on the floor earlier. *Bloody hell.* I forgot to move them because I haven't had a single second to think about anything. I stumble again as I try to climb over the books, but I wind up sprawled on top of them instead.

"Never mind," the testy woman says. "I'll go to another bookshop."

I scramble to get to my feet, but instead, drop onto my arse. A lock of hair has fallen over my eyes, and I try to blow it away. But the hair falls over my eyes again.

More customers enter the shop.

No, no, no more people. I will die if I have to serve more ravenous book lovers. For a moment, I simply sit here balanced on a stack of books and stare at my own feet. At least my shoes haven't been damaged. Lord Sommerleigh gave me these Oxfords for Christmas last year.

If I close my eyes and wish with all my might, will I awaken to find I'm back at Sommerleigh, far from this madness?

After a moment, I push myself up and approach the counter again. Then I brush my hair back, square my shoulders, and do what any good Englishman would. I get my chin up and soldier on.

The door swings open, and I nearly pass out when I see who has entered the shop. It's Owen Metzger and Poppy Goodburn. Reinforcements have arrived at last. I pray Poppy won't be horrified by the state of her beloved bookshop, but I've done the best I could. When Lord Sommerleigh asked me to care for the shop in Poppy's absence, I had thought it would be…less nightmarish.

Five days of running a bookshop had seemed feasible.

No, it is *not*.

Poppy has rung the shop every day to check on me, and she undoubtedly worries I will chase people away or burn down the building. I might be rubbish at operating a business, but I would never do anything to harm the bookshop or Poppy's bottom line. Well, I wouldn't do that intentionally.

My relief at seeing Poppy and Owen spurs me to do a bloody stupid thing. I wave my arms about like a lunatic and shout, "Ma'am! Miss Goodburn, ma'am!"

What, do I expect she won't notice me unless I scream?

In my haste to greet Poppy and Owen, I lean forward and continue waving my arms. A book topples to the floor. At last, they hurry over here.

Poppy's eyes are wide. "Kendall, my goodness. Are you all right?"

"No, ma'am, I'm not. Forgive me for saying so."

"What's wrong?"

I glance round the shop and grimace. "I don't have the temperament for running a bookshop. People keep coming in and wanting to buy things. It hasn't stopped since we opened this morning."

Owen and Poppy glance at each other and nod, as if they've reached a mutual decision via telepathy.

Poppy rushes behind the counter and shoos me away. "Sit down and rest, love. You're overworked. Owen and I can handle the bookshop today."

Oh, thank goodness. I slump onto a chair and blow hair away from my eyes again. "Bugger me, Miss Goodburn. I have no idea how you do this every day. May I please go home to Sommerleigh?"

"Yes, of course. Owen, why don't you call Hugh and ask him to send a car for Kendall?"

"Sure thing," her American beau says.

I can't even focus on what Owen says once he gets hold of Lord Sommerleigh. Relief has flooded through me so forcefully that I've become a limp rag draped over this chair. Poppy gets to work, handling customers with finesse and cheerfulness whilst Owen deals with all the books on the counter and the ones that had fallen onto the floor. I know how to tidy up. But my brain was not built for this sort of chaos.

Fifteen minutes later, a four-door Mercedes pulls up directly in front of the shop. I know that car. It belongs to Lord and Lady Sommerleigh.

I am saved.

Poppy hugs me and kisses my cheek, telling me that I had done a smashing job in her absence. It's rubbish, and we both know it. But I appreciate her desire to make me feel better. Owen slaps my arm and declares that I "rocked the bookshop." I only did that if "rocking" means that I tripped over books and knocked down tables, creating a thumping noise like a rock falling.

As I shuffle toward the door with my head bowed, a sense of extreme relief rushes through me. But then movement catches my attention, and I look up at the person who just entered the shop—and I freeze. A beautiful ginger-haired woman stands in front of me, though her attention is focused on the tables of books around her. Whilst she bites her lip, seeming confused, I can do nothing but stare at her face and the faint freckles on her creamy skin. When she turns toward me, her green eyes shimmer like polished emeralds.

The girl turns toward me a little too far and stumbles into me. Our bodies meet for the briefest moment, but it's enough to make my pulse accelerate and my breaths quicken. She is the loveliest woman I have ever seen. She even smells good, though not as if she wears perfume. It's simply her natural scent.

And it's intoxicating.

She flashes me a quick, apologetic smile before she brushes past me.

I shuffle round to keep her in my sight, though I can't move from this spot. Her hips sway slightly. Her shapely arse entrances me, and I flash back to a moment ago when her breasts had brushed against me for a split second. Whilst I gawp at her, she repeatedly glances back at me with the sweetest shy smile playing on her lips.

Then another bloke bumps into her, and I lose sight of the girl as even more book lovers enter the shop.

Well, a woman like that would never date a man like me, anyway.

I trudge outside and stop at the rear door of the Mercedes, hesitating for reasons I cannot fathom. Are my employers in the car? I won't know until I move my ruddy arse. Finally, I convince myself to pull the car door open.

The interior is empty.

Relief rushes through me. I love Lord and Lady Sommerleigh, but I can't bear to see anyone after my ordeal this week at the bookshop.

I've just settled onto the plush leather seat in the Mercedes when the shop door swings open. The movement catches my attention, and I glance in that direction. Even through the tinted window, I can tell who that person is. The woman who made my heart race has just dropped her small purse and bends over to pick it up. That action makes her blouse fall open a bit. I get a glimpse of the slopes of her breasts, and it makes my mouth water.

She straightens, clearly about to walk away.

And I lose my mind. That's the only explanation for what I do next. I swing the door open and call out to her. "Miss? I say, miss?"

The beautiful girl surveys the area, clearly confused.

"Oy! Over here, miss." I flap my hand in an attempt to gain her attention.

She finally looks my way—and grins. "Oh, hi, it's you again."

"Do you need a ride? I'd be happy to drop you wherever you're going."

The beauty bites her lip. "Not sure if I should do that. You seem nice enough, but I don't know you."

"My name is Kendall. Does that help? I work for Lord and Lady Sommerleigh."

"Don't know who they are." She inches closer to the car, bending over to peer inside. That means I enjoy another glorious view of her cleavage. "I have learned to trust my instincts, though. And I hate taxis. Buses are even worse."

"Are you considering my offer of a ride, then?"

"No, I'm not considering it." She leaps over me to land on the other side of the bench seat. "I've decided. You're cute and sweet, and I trust you not to murder me."

"Ah, thank you, I suppose." That might be the oddest compliment I've ever received. Actually, it might be the only one I've ever received. I pull the door shut. "Where should I take you?"

Her smile turns a touch wicked. "Now that's a loaded question."

This beautiful woman can't be flirting with me. That never happens.

She pats my thigh. "That was a joke, sweetie."

"Ah, yes, I thought it must be."

"I'm flying home today, so you can drop me off at Gatwick Airport."

"Did you hear that, Arthur?" The driver mumbles something that I take for an affirmative response. The car starts rolling down the street, and I face the woman who sits beside me. "What's your name? I told you mine, so it's only fair that I know yours."

"I'm Rachelle." She offers me her hand to shake. "Nice to meet you, Kendall. I love your accent, by the way. This is my first time in the UK, and you're my favorite person I've met here."

"You are definitely my favorite person I have ever met in my entire life."

Oh, bollocks. That sounded desperate and pathetic, didn't it? I'm too old to behave like a schoolboy. But this woman makes me feel exactly like that.

Rachelle grins and laughs, though it sounds affectionate rather than mocking. "You're just the cutest. I wish I could spend more time with you. But like I said, I'm flying home in a few hours. Need to get to the airport."

All my hopes have just been dashed. But I will do what I promised and give her a ride. "Arthur, our guest needs to go to the airport."

"Sure thing, Kendall."

Rachelle sidles closer to me until our thighs meet. "Are you the big boss? I mean, you have this fancy car."

"It belongs to Lord and Lady Sommerleigh. I'm their butler, but this week I've been filling in at the bookshop for Poppy Goodburn. She's a mate of my employers." I wince. "So, you see, I am not a celebrity or a member of the peerage."

"Are you expecting me to run away because you're a normal guy? I'm not that shallow."

"Sorry. I didn't mean—"

Rachelle seals my lips with her finger. "It's okay. I get nervous too when I meet someone new, especially if it's a guy who gives me warm shivers."

I feel that way too, but I won't admit that to her. Though I have never been the forward sort, I can't stop myself from leaning toward her and lowering my voice to a deeper register. "Arthur, could you raise the partition, please?"

Out of the corner of my eye, I can see Arthur's faint smirk. He winks and raises the partition. Rachelle and I are now alone.

I lay a hand on her cheek, then slide it up until my fingers dive into her hair. I've never felt anything as soft or smelled anything as intoxicating. "Would you mind if I kissed you?"

"Please do. I've never done anything like this before, but I would absolutely love to feel your lips on mine."

"As would I."

While her lids flutter shut, I lean in even more until our lips meet. For a moment, we both remain motionless and seem not to even breathe. Then she issues the sweetest little moan, and I can't hold back any longer. I tug her closer and crush my mouth to hers while I slip my tongue between her lips. Though I made no conscious decision to do it, I wrap my free arm around her waist and pull her even closer until her tits are mashed against my chest. She tastes like cinnamon and caramel with a hint of chocolate, and the flavor drives me mad.

That simple taste pushes me over the edge. I consume her with abandon, and she does the same. Our tongues tangle, and she climbs onto my lap, emitting faint grunting noises that make me even randier. She rocks her hips into me while I fling both my arms around her and shamelessly grope her body. The heat of our kissing flares into a wildfire, melting my common sense, and I transform into a man I don't recognize, yet it feels fucking fantastic.

The trip from Croydon to Gatwick seems to take a matter of moments, as if time has frozen inside the bubble of the backseat. Something happens then, and for months afterward, I will have trouble believing I did that thing on this day. By the time it's over, Rachelle and I can't manage to look at each other and certainly can't speak.

Then the sound of the partition lowering penetrates my lust-drunk mind.

Arthur clears his throat. "We're at Gatwick, Kendall."

Rachelle leaps off my lap and straightens her clothes.

I'm struggling to catch my breath. But I can see that Arthur only lowered the partition a couple of inches, ever the tactful driver. Our employers would be proud. Well, not if they knew how I'd behaved inside their car.

"Thank you for the lift," Rachelle says as she crawls over me and pushes the door open. Then she hops out of the car, turning to smile at me. That expression could light up the whole city. "I wish we could've gotten to know each other, but I have to go home. You're the sweetest, and I'm so glad I had this experience with you. Goodbye, Kendall."

She rushes into the terminal.

By the time my brain has processed what just happened, it's too late. I can't dash into the terminal to find her. I have no boarding pass.

"Should we leave now?" Arthur asks.

"Yes. Let's go home."

For the first time in my life, I've met a woman who makes me feel…everything. But I will never see her again. I don't even know how to spell her first name, though she pronounced it Ruh-SHELL. I'll go back to being just Kendall, the butler.

I sink back into my seat and sigh.

Chapter One

Rachelle
Four months Later

An airline employee hands my boarding pass back to me and gives me a polite smile. "Thank you for flying with us. We hope you have a smooth journey and a wonderful holiday in the UK. Please take a seat and wait for the boarding call."

I smile. "Thank you. I'm excited to visit London again."

The woman's lilting British accent reminds me of someone I met four months ago, someone I know I will never see again, though I want to see him. Want it so much. As I turn away from the counter and trudge over to a chair that looks as uncomfortable as I'm sure it will feel, my thoughts travel back in time.

Closing my eyes, I picture Kendall.

Maybe I met the man once and spent less than an hour with him, total, including our encounter in the bookshop. Most of that time elapsed inside that Mercedes with the partition up and our inhibitions down. Destroyed, actually. I lost every last shred of my common sense with Kendall. Still can't quite believe what I did.

The boarding agent calls for passengers to begin boarding.

I lug my wheeled suitcase down the jet bridge with my duffel bag slung over my shoulder. Jeez, it's heavy. I overpacked, for sure, but it's too late to worry about that. Somehow, I manage to stuff my luggage into the overhead bins inside the airplane. Nobody gives me any dirty looks. Thank goodness for that. I settle onto my assigned seat, which is so cramped I think I might need a winch to get me out of it. Then I wince as my fellow passengers push past me to get into their seats. I'm crushed between them.

Oh yeah, I love commercial air travel.

My cell phone goes bloopety-bloop, indicating a new text. I sheepishly glance at my seatmates, but they're too busy staring at their own phones to notice.

The text is from my dad. *Bon voyage, sweetie. Have a good time in London.*

I type my response: *Thanks. I'll send you a postcard and email plenty of pics.*

He replies with a thumbs-up emoji.

Dad isn't great with technology, but he has embraced texting and email. He only started using emojis last year, but he got totally on board with that right away. I feel guilty for leaving him alone at home. Despite his assurances that he can do fine on his own, I suffer a moment of guilt-ridden panic. It passes quickly, thank heavens. I can't help thinking back on what he'd said when I mentioned I'd love to visit the UK again.

"Go ahead and do it, pumpkin. You deserve a vacation, and the one a few months ago ended early because of me. I'm fine now. So go on, make the airline reservation." He winked. "That guy you met must be dying to see you again."

"Dad, I spent less than an hour with him. It's not true love."

"Give it a shot. Your bad luck with men might just have ended."

So yeah, that's how I wound up on this plane. The girl from Columbia, Missouri, is returning to the scene of the crime in London, England.

With a ten-hour flight ahead of me, I have nothing to do except sleep and think. I'd brought a book with me, but reading gets tedious after a few hours. I play games on my phone until I start to go cross-eyed. Then I try to watch the in-flight movie, but it's terrible. I fill the time in the most inappropriate way. What if someone figures out what I'm fantasizing about? *Oh please.* No one will realize I'm having dirty fantasies about a British man I met once. And yes, I'm returning to England because I hope to see

Kendall again. It's insane, but I don't care. My own father encouraged my lunacy.

Settling back in my seat, I fold my hands on my lap and let my mind show me a replay of those forty minutes inside a spiffy Mercedes with the privacy partition rolled up.

"Wake up, lady. You're holding up the deboarding."

A strong pair of hands shake me roughly.

I rouse from my fantasy, which had turned into the hottest dream ever when I apparently nodded off. Yawning, I rub my eyes and wipe away the saliva that had dribbled down my chin. "Sorry. I didn't mean to fall asleep."

The guy who shook me, and who sits in the seat next to mine, snorts and gives me a nasty look. "Just get off your ass. We all want to deboard."

Who calls it "deboarding"? Only flight attendants, as far as I know.

But I give the rude man a pleasant smile and apologize yet again. Then, we finally exit the plane. Fortunately, I had booked a rental car in advance, and it's waiting for me. I rely on the maps app on my phone to get me to my first destination. No, it's not a hotel. I'll check in there later. First, I need to make another stop. I have to park a block away, behind another building, but that gives me the chance to change out of my flight clothes and into a pretty dress. After that brief walk, I finally reach my destination.

I'm standing outside, staring at the glass door that says, "Goodburn's Literary Treasures." This is the bookshop where I met Kendall.

Should I go inside? Well, duh, that's why I flew all the way to London. To see Kendall. What are the odds he'll be here? Someone else owns the shop, a woman called Poppy Goodburn. Maybe she will know where I can find the man I've come all this way to see.

What if he thinks I'm stalking him?

The door swings open, and a couple walks out. The man has his arm draped over the woman's shoulders. They smile and nod as they pass by me.

No more vacillating. I square my shoulders, lift my chin, and march into the bookshop.

Then I freeze just past the door, while it swings shut behind me. Can't think. Can't move.

Four people stand at the sales counter, two men and two women, with one couple on this side of the counter and the other pair behind it. Three of them are engaged in a lively conversation and haven't noticed me yet. Since there are customers wandering through the shop, it's hardly surprising that the proprietor hasn't seen me yet, and I certainly don't expect her to remember me.

The fourth person, an attractive man, does notice my arrival. "Good afternoon. Do you need help finding a book? My cousin Poppy can help you, or her fiancé Owen could do. Those are the two people behind the counter."

I bite my lip, suddenly uncertain of what to do next.

Poppy and Owen abruptly look at me. She smiles brightly. "Hello, it's you, Rachelle. Isn't it?"

How does she know my name? *Oh, duh.* Kendall must have told her.

She waves to me. "Come over here, Rachelle, please."

I traipse over there, halting between the man who had called out to me and the pretty woman beside him. "Hi there."

The man offers me his hand to shake. "Dominic Rigby. And this is my wife, Chelsea. She's American like you and Owen."

"Really? Do a lot of Brits marry Americans?"

"No idea. But among my mates and relatives, it's become common."

"Oh, I see." Must be my turn to introduce myself. "I'm Rachelle Buckholtz."

Poppy rushes around the counter to pull me into a brief hug. "We're all so chuffed to see you again. I'm Poppy Goodburn, and that handsome bloke behind the counter is Owen Metzger."

"And he's engaged to you, right?"

"Yes." Poppy smiles with her lips sealed, clearly excited that I'm here. "You've come back to find Kendall, haven't you?"

Well, I guess it wasn't that hard for her to figure out my motivation. But I am surprised that she and Owen remember me. I was in this shop for five minutes, tops, and it had been very busy on that day. What if Kendall told them about our time in the

Mercedes? No, he wouldn't do that. I have no idea why, but I'm convinced of his decency.

"Let's ring Hugh," Dominic says. "He can tell Kendall his girl has come back for him."

"That's a wonderful idea," Poppy says. "A reunion would be lovely."

Owen reaches across the counter to grasp his fiancée's hand. "Take it easy, baby. You're scaring Rachelle."

My eyes might be bulging right now. I'm not scared of these people, but I am starting to feel weird about this whole vacation-in-London idea. What are the odds that Kendall will want to see me again? He's probably forgotten all about me.

Chelsea approaches me. "Relax, hon, we aren't going to kidnap you. Dom and Poppy are just happy to see you again, especially since Kendall won't talk about you at all. That's how we know he desperately does want to see you."

Uh, sure, that made sense.

I back away two steps. "Maybe I should go. This is all getting a little weird."

Chelsea studies me for a moment with her head tipped to the side. "You came here to find him, didn't you?"

"Well, uh…maybe?" I suddenly realize I'm biting my lip so hard it hurts a little bit. "This was a crazy idea. I shouldn't have flown from Missouri to England just to find some guy I met once for forty minutes."

"The fact that you know how many minutes you were with him suggests you do desperately want to see Kendall." She pats my arm. "It's nothing to be ashamed of. Kendall isn't the effusive type, but we've learned to interpret his facial expressions. Whenever someone mentions you, he gets a look on his face that means he wishes he could find you."

"Sure, if you say so."

Poppy trots over to us. "Why don't I ring Hugh? He can ask if Kendall wants to see you. If he does…we'll go from there. All right?"

"Um, sure."

Maybe I should just go to my hotel and wait for the next available seat on an airline flight. But I don't want to leave without seeing Kendall again. Have I become obsessed with him? Jeez, I hope not. The honest truth is that I've never felt anything like what I experienced when I first saw Kendall or when we did those things in that car.

Poppy goes into a back room to make her call, returning a few minutes later. "Hugh said he needs to break the news gently so that Kendall won't panic. Honestly, I cannot picture him panicking." She winces. "Though he did get quite frazzled when I left him in charge of the bookshop. But that was a one-off reaction."

I remember that day, but I had arrived after whatever 'frazzled' things Kendall had done. When I bumped into him, literally, he had smiled at me in the sweetest way. My heart thudded in that moment. I felt a rush of excitement, and suddenly, I started to wonder if instant attraction might be a real thing.

"What should I do while we wait?" I ask. "Who knows how long it'll take for your friend to talk to Kendall."

Dominic chuckles. "It won't take long at all, trust me. Once the American Wives Club get involved, events unfold swiftly."

"The what club?" I swear, if these people are trying to drag me into a kinky sex club situation, I'll run out of this shop so fast that they won't even see me.

Poppy reaches across the counter to touch my hand. "Don't worry, Rachelle, it's nothing sinister. The American Wives Club is all about meddling to help couples discover if they're meant for each other."

"Uh-huh. Not sure that's as comforting as you think. You guys are strangers to me."

"I know, pet, but give us a chance. You'll see we only want the best for you and for Kendall." The distinctive sound of a text message pinging someone's phone echoes through the shop, and Poppy grins as she reads the text. "Wonderful news! Hugh says Kendall wants to see you. Lord and Lady Sommerleigh will escort him to the shop, so we should all wait here."

"I sort of remember hearing those names before. Sommerleigh is their last name, I guess?"

"No, it's their shared title. Hugh Parrish is a viscount. That means he and his wife, Avery, are called Lord and Lady."

I probably shouldn't ask because I do not understand the British aristocracy, but morbid curiosity takes hold. "Um, if Hugh's last name is Parrish, why do you call him Lord Sommerleigh?"

"None of this rubbish makes any sense, does it?" Dominic says. "You'll get used to it if you stay in England long enough. Frankly, even many Brits don't understand the etiquette of the peerage."

Well, at least I'm not alone in my utter confusion.

Owen comes up beside Poppy and slings an arm around her waist, though he looks at me. "As a fellow American, I can tell you that a lot of the words that come out of British mouths will sound like gibberish to you. Eventually, though, you'll come to appreciate Brit-speak. These people have the cutest ways of describing things. They call it the 'round-the-houses' method or something like that."

I'm apparently receiving a crash course in British-isms and aristocratic etiquette. It's interesting, but I have trouble focusing on the conversation because my heart sped up the moment I heard that Kendall might be here soon. "How long will it take for your friends to bring Kendall here?"

"Sommerleigh is about two and a half hours away."

All my excitement wilts like a flower in the hot sun. Two and a half hours? What am I going to do until then? "Guess I should go check in at my hotel. I haven't done that yet. If someone could hail me a taxi—"

"Nonsense," Poppy declares. "Owen and I will drive you to your hotel, then take you to our favorite fish and chips shop."

"I have a rental car."

"But you won't need it, pet. Please, let us show you round and be your chauffeurs. You can call the car hire agency to have them retrieve your car."

Accepting a ride from these people wouldn't be the craziest thing I've ever done, not by a long shot. "Okay. That's very kind of you. But who will run your bookshop while we're gone?"

"It's gone five. That means it's closing time. Hadn't you noticed that all the customers have left?"

Glancing around, I realize the shop is empty now—and I feel like a moron for not noticing that. "Oh, yeah, right. In that case, I accept your hospitality."

Poppy grins. "Brilliant!"

I can't imagine why a stranger would be thrilled to escort me to my hotel and buy me food, but whatever.

Dominic and Chelsea decide to stay in the shop in case Lord and Lady Sommerleigh arrive earlier than expected. Poppy and Owen drive me to my hotel in the tiniest car I've ever seen. It's adorable, and the seats are surprisingly comfortable, but I feel like I'll need a crowbar wielded by two brawny men to get me in and out of the vehicle. The car I drive back home isn't huge, but it seems monstrous in comparison with Poppy's little tin can.

Her favorite fish and chips shop offers yummy food. It's possible I'm just so hungry after a long, long flight to the UK that even my napkin looks appetizing. But I decide to assume the food is good.

When we return to the bookshop, the sun has already set and only vestiges of its glow feather out across the lowest portions of the sky. Dominic and Chelsea are sitting at the sales counter playing some kind of card game. They stop when we walk in and the bell above the door jingles. When they ask how I liked my hotel and the fish and chips, I assure them both that the food was yummy and the hotel is pretty good.

Dominic's brows lift. "Pretty good? Oh, you poor thing. You need an upgrade, American Wives Club style. A beautiful woman should never languish in a mediocre hotel."

"I'm fine with the place I booked. Really."

Owen grabs a book off a table and hands it to me. "Here's what you really need. It's the latest Desiree Lachance novel, full of steam and heart and humor. Free of charge, for a new friend."

"That's very sweet, but it's unnecessary."

He picks up my hand, placing the book in my palm. "I wrote this novel, and I insist you take it. If you want to toss it into the nearest garbage can later, go for it."

"You write steamy romance novels?"

"That's right. Desiree Lachance is my pen name."

I'd love to talk to Owen more about his career, but the doorbell jingles, and we all turn to face the three people who just walked into the shop. A couple who are holding hands step inside first, then another person appears. And my heart shifts into overdrive, making me feel giddy and lightheaded.

Why? Because Kendall just entered the bookshop.

Chapter Two

Kendall

As I step inside the shop, and my employers move aside, I finally get a good look at the woman who traveled all this way to see me. That can't be right. No one would fly thousands of miles to find me, a simple butler. And there is absolutely no way on earth that a woman as beautiful as Rachelle would do that. Yet here she is. In the flesh. I'm not hallucinating, am I? No, if I were imagining this moment, Rachelle and I would be alone.

And naked, preferably.

Just thinking that word—naked—makes my mind flash back to four months ago in the Mercedes with Rachelle. I still can't believe what we did. But I don't regret it.

Poppy gives Rachelle a gentle shove, which makes her stumble forward a couple of paces. She bites her lip and hunches her shoulders. I have a feeling I'm doing the same thing. My pulse has accelerated, and my palms have grown moist. I have trouble pulling in a full breath too.

After what feels like days but was probably thirty seconds, I manage to speak. "Hello, Rachelle. It's, ah, lovely to see you again."

"Nice to see you too."

I suppose we might make this moment more awkward if we tried very, very hard. But I rather doubt it. Why had I let Lord and Lady Sommerleigh talk me into coming all the way to Croydon to meet with a girl I knew for forty-five minutes, four months ago. Forty of those minutes elapsed inside the Mercedes. I still can't believe what we did—what I did—in the backseat with Rachelle.

She bites her lip, and her forehead wrinkles. "Are you okay, Kendall?"

"Ah…"

Panic rises inside me as I suddenly realize I cannot speak to her. I'm physically capable of doing that, but the ramifications could be…catastrophic. I'm bloody awful at conversation, especially with a woman and most especially with her. The way I'm gawping at her proves that point. I have only one option.

I clear my throat. "Sorry. I don't think this is a good idea."

Then I turn on my heels and walk out the door, halting inches away from the car.

Lord Sommerleigh races after me. "Kendall, what in the world are you doing? We brought you here so you could reunite with Rachelle."

"I know, sir. Sorry, sir." I grimace and scratch inside the collar of my shirt, though I don't feel itchy. "I do not wish to reunite. Sorry, sir."

Maybe I do want to spend more time with Rachelle, but it would end in disaster. I've gone down this road before, and I wound up lying in a ditch naked with my body akimbo. Well, not literally. That was a stupid metaphor. Luckily, no one can hear my thoughts.

I might be the only person on earth who would ever use the word akimbo.

"Sorry, sir, Lord Sommerleigh, sir."

He places a hand on my shoulder. "Please stop apologizing, Kendall. You want to talk to Rachelle, don't you?"

I shrug. It's all I can manage to do.

"Why are you afraid to speak to her?"

"Not sure, sir. Sorry, sir."

He shuts his eyes and sighs, then looks at me. "How many times have I asked you to call me Hugh? And you know Avery would love for you to use her first name too. You're family, Kendall."

"Uh, thank you, sir. Hugh, sir." I might have winced when I spoke his first name. I have never referred to him that way before.

He shakes his head and sighs. "All right, go on calling me Lord Sommerleigh."

"Oh, thank goodness." I realize what I've said, and my eyes go wide for a split second. "Sorry, sir. I meant—"

"Relax. We won't force you to spend time with the beautiful, sweet woman who flew all the way here from America to see you."

Yes, I am a coward. But she couldn't possibly understand why I panic every time I think about what we did four months ago. Perhaps I simply need time to adjust to this new situation.

A figure emerges from the shop, but I only see the person peripherally. Lord Sommerleigh and I are facing away from the building.

My employer glances over his shoulder and smirks. "Afraid you'll need to handle this on your own."

He turns to head back into the shop.

I rotate my head just enough that I can tell who is standing behind me. My first instinct is to leap into the car and order Arthur to break the speed laws to get me home to Sommerleigh as quickly as possible. But I have never been a coward, not until today. I can't explain my behavior—not now, and certainly not four months ago.

No, I will not run away.

So, I straighten my jacket and face the woman. "I apologize, Rachelle. I shouldn't have run away."

"No need to apologize. I shouldn't have ambushed you like this."

"You are not to blame."

She inches closer. "Of course I am. I'm the one who jumped out of the car and ran into the airport terminal without even saying goodbye. You were so sweet, insisting on stopping so I could pick up my luggage, then dropping me off at the airport."

"Why did you run away so quickly?"

"Embarrassment, I suppose. I'd never done anything like that before."

I know she isn't talking about not saying goodbye. She means what happened in the car. Now, as I gaze into her eyes, I find myself moving closer to her. The cold panic I'd experienced a moment ago has melted into a silky warmth. She's so lovely, so sweet, and she tastes like the most decadent dessert on earth, from her lips down to her... No, I shouldn't think about that right now.

Her eyes have grown large, and they shimmer with the richest shade of emerald I've ever seen. That's probably because her pupils have dilated. She inches toward me again, and I do the same, as if an industrial magnet draws us toward each other. "Ever since I went home, I haven't been able to stop thinking about you."

"I've thought of nothing else but you since that day." Why has my voice grown deeper? It's rubbish. "Despite my behavior a moment ago, I've done little else over the past four months other than thinking about you."

"Ditto for me."

"But, we, ah, shouldn't do that again. The thing we did in the car, that is."

Her lips curl into the loveliest little smile. "Why not? It was incredible."

"I am not who you think I am."

"You're a butler. I know that." She tentatively slips her hand into mine. "I don't care about that. Do you really think I'm so shallow that I'd look down on you for not having a high-powered job?"

"No, of course not. But that isn't what I meant." I pull my hand away. "Please, I think it's best if we part ways. It's been lovely to see you again, and I hope you have a pleasant holiday here in London."

Turning away from her, I pull the car door open.

"Wait, Kendall, please."

I climb into the Mercedes.

But before I can shut the door, Rachelle leans in. "If you change your mind, all your friends know where I'm staying."

I nod curtly while staring out the windscreen.

The door shuts, but the car does not begin to roll down the street. Instead, Arthur lowers the partition and gives me a stern look. "What's wrong with you, mate? A pretty girl wants you and practically begs you to date her. But you just get in the car and don't say a word."

"My behavior is no one's concern but mine."

"No more 'sorry, sir, no sir,' eh?"

"Sorry, Arthur. I didn't mean to insult you."

He shakes his head, much the way Lord Sommerleigh had done. Then Arthur faces forward again, though he leaves the partition down.

"Can we go now?" I ask.

"Need to wait for the bosses."

"Oh. Yes, of course."

I hear the sound of a text message pinging, but I don't think it's mine. My suspicion is confirmed when Arthur raises his mobile.

He drops it onto the seat beside him. "His Nibs and Mrs. Nibs are staying on in London. We're to go home." Arthur twists his head round to squint at me. "But in my opinion, you and that girl should—"

"My personal life is private." I wince, which seems to have become a habit lately. "Sorry, Arthur. I didn't mean to be curt with you."

He sighs. "I don't understand you. After what you and that girl did in the backseat last time she was here—"

I jerk forward. "Did you hear all of that?"

Arthur chuckles. "Oh, yeah, mate. I've got ears, you know, and the partition isn't soundproof."

"Oh, bollocks." I slump against the seat and sink down until I'm slouching so far that I might slide off the smooth leather. "Did you tell anyone about that?"

He winks. " 'Course not. What kind of bloke do you take me for? We both work for His Nibs and Mrs. Nibs, which means we're trustworthy."

Of course we are. That's what people like us do. We keep our employers' confidences, though Lord and Lady Sommerleigh have no deep, dark secrets that we need to keep for them. They are the kindest, most honorable people I've ever known. Perhaps Lord Sommerleigh did have a bit of a reputation before he met the woman who would become his viscountess. The ladies used to call him Lord Steamy, after all. But he has grown into the viscount that his father would have wanted him to be.

Lord and Lady Sommerleigh step into the car, both giving me pitying looks. Then Arthur drives us home.

That night, I can't get to sleep. I toss and turn in the most clichéd manner, my restlessness causing me to sweat. All right, perhaps it isn't only my movements that do that. I also grow warm and slightly sweaty because of my fantasies. The memory of that day four months ago won't let go of me. What else can I do? If I can't sleep, I might as well relive those forty minutes in the Mercedes.

As I close my eyes, I allow the memories to flood through me, and I swear every sensation comes back to me too as if I'm there, in the moment.

Rachelle is on my lap, rocking her hips into my thickening erection while I grope every inch of her body, from the nape of her neck down to her arse. Every time she thrusts her hips forward, she moans in the most suggestive manner. We're practically fucking. The scent of her desire fills the backseat. Bloody hell, I shouldn't be doing this, but I can't stop myself. I need more of her, all of her, right now.

Without relinquishing her lips, I shove my hand under her frock and grip her knickers, then yank them so hard that the fabric splits apart. Rachelle moans into my mouth. I unzip my trousers and free my cock. Somewhere in the recesses of my mind, I know I shouldn't be doing this. It's reckless, and I am never like that. But this woman, who I met moments ago, has inflamed something in me that I never knew I possessed—sheer, unadulterated lust.

I pull my mouth away just long enough to ask a question. "Are you sure you want this?"

"Yes, Kendall, yes." She drags her tongue over her lips, then grasps my cock. "Please don't stop."

"Couldn't if I wanted to, not after you begged me to keep going."

I toss her knickers away and thrust my hand between her legs, rubbing her cleft with my whole hand. She gasps and resumes rocking her hips, into my waiting palm this time. Her cream covers my hand, dribbling between my fingers while I rub harder and faster and she lets out sharp staccato cries. I should have worried about what Arthur might hear, but the thought never entered my mind.

Because I was obsessed with entering *her*.

Rachelle throws her head back. "Need you inside me now, Kendall."

Can't respond, not with words. My cock feels like it's about to explode from the pressure of my lust for this woman I met minutes ago. She loves what I'm doing to her so much that she rises to her knees and begins to rotate her hips while I plunge one finger into her sheath, followed by another, and another, until I've got all my fingers buried inside her. Her breaths come rapid-fire, just like mine.

I lunge my head forward to take her nipple into my mouth and suck. She grips my shoulders while I keep fucking her with my hand. Then I push her frock up, over her hips, and higher still until I've exposed her tits. Then I seal my mouth around one stiff, rosy peak so I can ravish it thoroughly. *Stop*, a voice in the back of my mind urges. But the thought sounds like gibberish.

Bloody hell. I need to shag her with my cock, not just my hand.

I wrap my arms around Rachelle and flip us both over so she lies beneath me, spread out on the bench seat. Then I peel the frock off her body and shed my suit jacket.

"Need all of you naked, Kendall, please."

Can't resist anything she wants. I strip off all my clothes, tossing them wildly, having no bloody clue where the garments wind up. For several seconds, I simply gaze down at her beautiful, sensual, shapely, and delicious body lying there spread out beneath me while she bites her lip and releases it ever-so-slowly. But when she glides her palms up her belly and over her tits, I lose the last shred of my self-control.

I grasp her hips and lift them, then thrust inside her so deeply that I swear I can feel the tip of my cock nudging the top of her vagina. Don't care. Can't think. Nothing penetrates my mind except for thoughts of the best ways to shag this woman. I pummel her wildly while she claws at my chest and shoulders, letting out sharp whimpers while I grunt and groan.

Rachelle slings her legs around my hips.

I slap my hands down on the seat.

She catches my lip between her teeth and sucks on it.

And I go mad, fucking her so fiercely and wildly that I assume the car must be rocking too and we'll careen off the road at any second. But when she tugs on my balls, I know I'll come soon—and I need to ensure she goes there first. So, I rub her clit ruthlessly until she freezes and her back bows upward. Her mouth falls open, and I know she will scream when she comes.

I seal my mouth over hers and thrust my tongue while I keep on shagging her like a maniac.

She screams into my mouth as the spasms of her climax grip me. But when she teases my balls again, I go off. While I release everything I have inside her, she keeps coming around my cock until we're both finished. I collapse on top of her, breathing too hard to speak. My ears are ringing too.

After a moment or two, I feel capable of speech. As I brush hair away from her eyes, I ask, "How do you feel, pet?"

"Fantastic. Never felt this good in my entire life." She bends one leg to nudge me with her knee. "Damn, I thought British men were supposed to be uptight. But you are the hottest guy I've ever been with, hands down."

"Have done this sort of thing before?"

"Screwing a guy five minutes after we met? No, this is a first for me."

I roll onto my side and absently paint circles on her belly with one finger. "I've never done anything like this before either. But I'm glad it happened. No one who knows me would believe I could be this wild."

"Yeah, you did seem kind of uptight earlier."

"I'm afraid that's my normal manner."

She tickles my lips with her finger. "I think you're wrong about that. Nobody who goes that wild during sex could be naturally uptight."

"Are we done yet?"

Rachelle raises onto her elbows and aims a sensual smile at me. "We still have about thirty minutes until we arrive at the airport."

"Are you saying you'd like to shag again? I definitely want that."

"So do I."

The wildness I discovered in this car hasn't left me yet, and I feel a powerful need to squeeze every last iota of carnal recklessness out of myself before I say goodbye to this woman.

She hoists herself up even more and runs her tongue over my bottom lip. "Anything you want, I want it too. Anything."

"I have an idea, but it's...unusual."

"Let's go for it."

And for the next twenty-eight minutes, we did just that. For a brief time, I became a different person. Rachelle will be disappointed when she realizes I am not that uninhibited man, not anymore.

And that's why I can't ever see her again.

Chapter Three

Rachelle

The next morning, I wake up inside my lonely little hotel room and try to shake off the dream I had last night. It involved Kendall. And yeah, it took place inside that Mercedes, in the backseat with the partition rolled up. Seeing him again brought back all my memories of those forty minutes in a car with the hottest and most confusing man I've ever met. Kendall is an incredible lover, but he's also uptight and afraid to get to know me. He doesn't seem like the one-night-stand type, but then, I don't really know him.

I want to learn all about him, but he won't let me.

A thirty-nine-year-old woman shouldn't chase after a man like this. It's embarrassing. But after years of bad dates and worse relationships, I've had enough of the traditional method of dating. Might as well go crazy and stalk a perfectly sweet man.

I should get on a plane and fly home. Yep, that's what I will do.

But a vision of Kendall explodes in my mind. Naturally, my brain decides I need a replay of those forty hot minutes and the incredible things Kendall did to me in that Mercedes. Sure, he screwed me on the backseat, and it was amazing. But after that… Damn, I'm getting hot and wet just remembering what we did.

Don't think about that. I mean it, girl, no reminiscing about the hot Brit who gave you the best orgasms ever.

"Ugh." I fling the covers off and rub my hands over my face. "This is crazy, woman, time to go home."

Yeah, talking to myself is not a good sign.

I woke up wet and achy, thanks to that dream, and I still can't shake off the tension of a thwarted orgasm. I never come in my dreams, no matter how hot they are. But this one has left me so turned on that I feel antsy. Well, Kendall did this to me. Why shouldn't he solve the problem he created? A quick, smokin' hot fantasy of him will get me off in no time.

We're in the car, the partition is up, and Kendall just fucked me on the bench seat so thoroughly that I think I might have actually left my body for a few seconds. We both agreed we wanted more. So, when he told me he had an unusual idea, I jumped up and down with glee—in my mind. If I had actually done that, poor Arthur would've lost control of the car and rolled it into a ditch.

I can't believe I never once felt weird about getting it on like crazed bunnies inside a car with a driver in the front seat. Sure, the partition hid us from Arthur's view, but he must have heard us. We weren't exactly quiet.

My mind takes me back to that moment right after our backseat shag. Yeah, I've adopted the British word for sex. It's so cute. But I don't want to think sweet thoughts right now. No, I desperately need a rockin' climax. The closest I can get to reliving that moment is in my fantasies. So, I roll onto my stomach and imagine Kendall doing that incredible, strange thing to me.

Mm, yeah, that'll do the trick.

I rub my clit and close my eyes, pretending it's Kendall doing that to me.

My cell phone rings.

Ugh. Who's calling me? Don't care. I am not stopping until I've taken care of my needs. I'll go crazy if I don't get off right now—or worse, I'll do something way too naughty with the butler who makes me come like an exploding star. That's not the way to start a…whatever it is I hope to have with Kendall.

My phone rings again.

I keep rubbing myself, and any second I'll hit that peak. Just a little more… "Oh, Kendall, yes."

A fist raps on the door.

"Go away!" I shout. "I'm busy."

That damn fist pounds on my door this time. "Wakey-wakey, pet. Lord and Lady Sommerleigh have come to whisk you away."

Oh, jeez, he's got to be kidding. It's seven a.m., and I'm on the verge of an orgasm.

More knocking rattles the door.

I roll over and moan like the pathetic lust-addled moron I am.

"There's no point in arguing," Hugh declares. "We won't give up until you emerge from your cocoon."

"He means it," Avery says. "Even I can't talk Hugh out of this."

I heave myself up and into a sitting position, yawning while I swing my legs over the edge. "Okay, fine, I give. But I need to take a shower and get dressed."

"Avery and I shall await your presence here in the hallway."

Do all aristocrats talk that way? Or is he being sarcastic? I met the man yesterday, so I can't say which option is true.

I take the quickest shower on record—at least for me—and blow dry my hair so fast that I think I should get an award for my speed in getting myself presentable. Yesterday, I'd worn a dress. But today, I choose a more casual outfit of jeans, a peasant top, and hiking boots. If Hugh and Avery are whisking me away to see Kendall, I'll need all my willpower and the barrier of clothes to stop myself from doing something insanely wild with him again. I'm wearing a bra with a front closure. Maybe I should switch to the type that hooks in the back. Men often have trouble with that kind of closure.

Sure, that will stop me from ripping my clothes off for him. I mean, it's not like I'll lose control the second I hear his sexy British accent.

Now that I'm presentable, I swing the door open. "Are you two trying to kidnap me?"

Hugh and Avery exchange amused looks, then Lady Sommerleigh speaks. "No, sweetie, we're only trying to help you and Kendall. He's anxious about seeing you again, though none of us can figure out why. We need to try something different."

"Precisely," Hugh says. "You are free to slam the door in our faces, but we hope you'll give our idea a chance."

"Uh-huh. What is your idea?"

Avery hooks her arm around Hugh's bicep. "It's kind of a show-and-tell sort of thing."

I set my hands on my hips. "Give me more of a clue than that, or I will not go anywhere with you people. You're basically strangers to me."

"This is all to help you and Kendall."

"Who is also basically a stranger." One I screwed like crazy four months ago. But I don't know much of anything about him.

Avery whispers something to Hugh, and he nods. She faces me again. "I'm a member of the American Wives Club, which is a group of friends and family who have made it our mission to help our unmarried friends find love."

"I'm not marrying anybody."

"Not yet. But who knows what might happen if you and Kendall have a real conversation? Maybe even go on a date?"

This is beginning to sound completely bonkers. "Will you and your friends be watching while Kendall and I go to dinner? This had better not be some kind of weird sex club where all of you will be spying while we get it on."

Hugh scoffs. "We are not voyeurs."

Of course they aren't. I met these two yesterday, but I could tell from the start that they're good people. "Sorry. I didn't mean to insult you guys. This is a very strange situation I've gotten myself into, though, and I'm not sure what to do."

Avery touches my arm. "You want to see Kendall again, right?"

"Yeah, I think I do."

"Then you have two choices. One, let us take you to Sommerleigh so you can see Kendall there. Or two, we can kidnap Kendall and bring him to you here."

"Isn't Sommerleigh two and a half hours away? I remember that Owen guy told me so."

"Yes, that's right. But Hugh and I will make the trip fun for you." She nudges her husband in the side. "Right, honey? You'll employ all your Lord Steamy charms to make sure Rachelle isn't bored out of her skull or considering her escape options."

"Oh, yes, I know how to entertain women." Lord Sommerleigh smiles, and the corners of his mouth curl into a devious slant. "But I suspect Kendall is the one who has the most intimate knowledge of how to entertain Rachelle."

Avery jabs her elbow into Hugh's side this time while giving him a reproving look. "Behave yourself. This is no time for Lord Steamy humor. Relax, Rachelle, my husband is just yanking your chain."

"Sure, I get that. But why do you call him Lord Steamy?"

"It's a long story. He used to be a big-time player before I tamed him."

Hugh opens his mouth, probably to complain about his wife's comment that she tamed him. But Avery slaps a hand over his mouth to stop him from speaking. Lord Sommerleigh's eyes narrow, and the faint lines around them suggest he's smiling under his wife's hand.

Watching the interactions between these two people makes me want to see Kendall even more. Not for sex. Well, not only for that. I mostly want to find out if we could develop the kind of relationship Hugh and Avery have. Dominic and Chelsea seem to have the same sort of dynamic. My parents weren't great relationship role models. I've always looked to other people for information about that. Maybe that explains why I'm chasing after a virtual stranger.

No, I don't think so. There's something about Kendall, something I can't describe or explain. I need to know if this is real or just an infatuation triggered by amazing car sex.

"Okay," I tell my new friends, "take me to Sommerleigh."

"Brilliant!" Hugh almost shouts while grinning. "Kendall will be much more at ease at Sommerleigh. He doesn't care for cities, especially the large ones."

"I prefer the rural lifestyle too. I tell everyone I live in Columbia, Missouri, but my home is actually in the country about five miles outside the city limits."

"Ah, so you do have something in common. That's perfect."

I grab my purse and shut the door to my room behind me. "Let's go."

Lord and Lady Sommerleigh lead the way out of the hotel and to their waiting car—which is a limousine. The backseat offers two facing benches. My new friends take the seat that faces backward, while I have the forward-facing one all to myself. Well, if I have to go on a two-and-a-half-hour drive, might as well travel in the lap of luxury.

Hugh and Avery are true to their word. They keep me entertained with stories about the wacky antics their friends have gotten up to, and they don't only talk about their British buddies. Hugh's best friend is a Scot, and most of his buddies have married Americans. I already knew Poppy and Dominic had done that, since I met Owen and Chelsea. But I am surprised that so many other Brits have fallen for Americans. When Hugh explains that he's met a ton of Scots thanks to having a Scottish "best mate," I can't help wondering if I'll ever meet any of those folks.

"Oh, I'd wager you will meet them, eventually," Hugh says when I voice my curiosity aloud. "Callum and I haven't seen each other in person for coming up on six weeks. I wouldn't be surprised if he and Kate come roaring up the drive on his Harley."

"He would ride a motorcycle all the way from Scotland?"

"They usually tow the Harley most of the way, then leave their pickup truck and trailer at a storage lot while they drive the rest of the way on the Harley."

I've never seen a Harley Davidson motorcycle in person, much less ridden on one. The idea of a Scottish biker seems…odd, I suppose. Will this Callum guy be wearing a kilt when he shows up at Sommerleigh? I don't get the chance to ask because Avery starts telling a great story about how her brother, Derek, met and fell for the British billionaire Diana Sangster. She became Diana Hahn when she married Derek, and he became a stepdad to her adopted daughter, who started out as Diana's niece. That story has a sad beginning but a happy ending. Pippa lost both her parents, and Diana became her guardian. Now, the three of them are a family.

When my new friends ask about my family history, I change the subject not so deftly. They're too polite to point out I did that.

Before I realize how much time has passed, we've arrived at Sommerleigh. A long gravel driveway takes us to Sommerleigh House, a boxy structure that somehow pulls off a stately Victorian aura despite the utilitarian style. When the straight driveway becomes semicircular, the rougher gravel fades away in favor of the more aristocratic pea gravel. Not sure if British people think pea gravel is a high-tone thing, but it seems that way to me. I've never seen so much of that stuff in one place. Sommerleigh has a carpet of pea gravel that crunches under our shoes as we exit the limo and climb the front steps.

One half of the double doors bursts open, and an older woman rushes out to drag Hugh into a firm hug. "My darling boy, you're home at last."

"We've only been gone for one day, Mum."

"I know. But I missed you and Avery terribly. There's no one to talk to."

"But you and Kendall have lovely chats."

She sighs, and her shoulders slump. "Not since he came home yesterday. The poor boy won't speak at all except to say 'your tea, ma'am' or 'shall I decant the wine, ma'am.' It's bloody depressing."

"You must be frazzled, Mum, if you're cursing in front of a stranger. That's not proper etiquette."

He said that with a touch of sarcasm, though he does seem genuinely surprised by his mother's use of a curse word. Is "bloody" as vulgar as "fuck"? Not sure. These people and their friends are the first Brits I've ever met.

"Oh, tosh," his mother says. "Now, Hugh, introduce me to this lovely woman. I assume she is Kendall's girl."

Hugh sets a hand on my shoulder. "Mum, allow me to introduce Rachelle Buckholtz. She is indeed the woman who flew all the way here from America to find Kendall. Rachelle, this is my mother, Rosalyn Parrish, also known as the Dowager Lady Sommerleigh."

His mom clasps both my hands. "Welcome to Sommerleigh, Rachelle. Kendall needs a good woman, and he is the best man any woman could hope to meet."

"Thank you. But I don't even know if he'll talk to me."

She leans in and winks. "Leave that to us, pet."

"Um, what should I call you? Viscountess? Mrs. Parrish?"

"Rosalyn will do. The Parrishes have never strictly adhered to the etiquette of the peerage. We aren't that uptight."

The Dowager Lady Sommerleigh steps backward and swivels her head to shout, "Kendall, dear, we need you."

Footsteps clap in the hallway behind her. I can't see into that space far enough to tell who is approaching, but I assume it's the man she just summoned. But the footsteps abruptly stop. I can make out only a human-shaped shadow behind Rosalyn.

She flaps her hand at the shadow person. "Don't stand there like a statue, love. Come out and greet your guest."

The other half of the door swings open.

Kendall scuffles across the threshold but stays several feet away. He avoids looking me in the eye and speaks to Rosalyn. "What might I do for you, ma'am?"

She sighs and glances at me. "I can't even convince him to use my first name."

Kendall stands ramrod straight and has no discernible expression. He might as well be a robot. But his eyes keep flicking toward me in minute movements.

"Do say hello to the poor girl," Rosalyn tells him. "She traveled all this way to see you, and the least you can do is offer her a bit of brandy in the solarium."

"I am working, ma'am. Sorry, ma'am, I didn't mean to—"

"Hush, Kendall. The girl won't bite you." Rosalyn's lips stretch into a closed-mouth smile that has a devious slant to it. "Well, she won't bite unless you ask her to do it, that is."

"Mum!" Hugh exclaims. "I've asked you not to say such things in my presence. It's unseemly."

She waves a dismissive hand. "Nonsense. An old woman can say whatever she likes."

Hugh shuts his eyes briefly, shaking his head the tiniest bit. "You are not *that* old, Mum."

I'm getting the impression that the Dowager Lady Sommerleigh has a wicked sense of humor. That makes me like her even more.

Rosalyn grasps my hand, then secures Kendall's too. "I shall escort you two into the solarium." As she walks into the hallway, dragging us along with her, she pauses to holler, "Someone get a bottle of brandy and bring it to the solarium, please."

A woman wearing a maid's uniform emerges from somewhere and grins at us. "Oh, how wonderful! Kendall's girl is finally here. I'll fetch that brandy, ma'am."

"Thank you, Beatrice."

Rosalyn escorts us to the solarium, which is a beautiful enclosed porch with tons of floor-to-ceiling windows that let in the sunshine and give us a great view of the patio and lawn. Our hostess insists that we sit at a small table, across from each other. Then she walks out the door.

I am alone with Kendall, and suddenly, I can't think of a thing to say.

Chapter Four

Kendall

Rachelle and I stare at each other across the table, both of us seeming to have lost our voices and any ability we had to communicate. She can't be pleased that Lord and Lady Sommerleigh waylaid her and spirited her away to the estate. I assume they gave her the option to walk away, but they might have inadvertently given Rachelle the impression that this visit was mandatory. The more likely reason she's here is because she chose to come, yet I cannot believe any woman would travel halfway round the world to see me.

I'm a ruddy butler, not a cricket star like Dominic Rigby or a publishing magnate like Richard Hunter. I'm certainly not a member of the Mithorian royal family like Bennett Montague.

The woman sitting across from me squirms in her seat. "Um… Hi, Kendall."

"Hello, Rachelle." Aren't we bloody fantastic at conversation? I sit up straighter in my chair and clear my throat. "I hope Lord and Lady Sommerleigh weren't overly insistent about encouraging you to come here."

"No, they haven't done that. And they entertained me with stories about their friends for the whole two-and-a-half-hour drive from London."

"Yes, they are excellent at that sort of thing." Unlike me. I'm bloody awful at conversation, a fact that she must have realized already. I still can't figure out why she flew here from America to see me, and my mind insists on coming up with a reason, one that I blurt out. "Are you pregnant?"

Rachelle stares at me blankly for a few seconds, then she bursts out laughing. "That's why you think I'm here?"

"Well, ah, no." I wince and scratch under my collar, which seems to have been washed in a poison ivy tincture. "We did behave recklessly in that car a few months ago, and I never thought to take measures."

Now her brows lift. "Measures? I guess you mean that you didn't use a condom. It's okay, Kendall, I'm on the pill."

"Of course. I should have realized. But still, I should have—"

The solarium door opens, and Arthur waltzes in carrying a tray laden with a bottle of brandy and two glasses, plus a few food items. He sets the lot down on the table and winks at me. "Here you go, Kendall. I'll make sure nobody bothers you two until you're done with whatever it is you're meaning to do."

"Why are you serving us? That isn't your job."

"Beatrice is taking a coffee break, so you get me instead." He spreads his hands, lifting his chin. "Shall I decant the brandy, Mr. Kendall, sir?"

My face has grown unusually warm. I can't be blushing. Not me. Not in front of Rachelle. "I can open the bottle, Arthur, thank you."

"Oh, no, sir, I can't have His Nibs Junior performing a menial task. I got my orders direct from His Nibs Senior." Arthur winks at Rachelle. "That means Lord Sommerleigh himself gave the command."

Since I clearly cannot stop him from continuing with his ridiculous charade, I watch while Arthur opens the bottle and pours a serving into each glass. Then, thankfully, he leaves. The term His Nibs is usually an insult, but Arthur has turned it into an endearment of sorts.

Rachelle gazes down at the food Arthur brought for us. "What are these little ball thingies?"

"Fried mac and cheese balls. And the strips beside that are chocolate-covered bacon. Lord Sommerleigh loves that rubbish."

"Have you tried any of these foods?"

"Only the mac and cheese."

She picks up a mac-and-cheese ball, then pops it into her mouth and takes her time devouring it. "Mm, yummy."

I grab one too and wolf it down. "Not the worst thing I've ever eaten."

"Why haven't you tried the chocolate-covered bacon?"

"Because it sounds revolting."

She consumes one of the strips. "You really should try this. It's extra yummy."

"Perhaps another time."

I pick up my brandy snifter, meaning to sip the drink, but I hesitate.

Rachelle has just tossed a mac-and-cheese ball into her mouth and now shoves a strip of chocolate-covered bacon in there too. She chews it all up and moans. "Oh, that is unbelievably good."

The noise she made, it sounded exactly like the moans I'd heard four months ago in the backseat of Lord Sommerleigh's car. *Wonderful.* Now my cock is getting hard.

The sexiest woman I've ever seen raises a bacon strip to my lips. "You have to try this, Kendall. It's mm-mm-mm so deliciously yummy, just like you."

I can't say no, since I can't speak. And I find myself wrapped up in the sensual web she has woven around me, unable to fight it. So, I part my lips and let her slide that bacon strip into my mouth. Something unfathomable happens then. I close my lips around her fingers and suck on them.

She pulls them out millimeter by millimeter while licking her lips.

My cock jerks. I have no choice but to consume the chocolate-covered bacon, then I down the other half of my brandy in one gulp.

Rachelle grins. "Slow down, cowboy. This isn't a drinking contest at a Wild West saloon."

"Sorry."

"You don't need to keep apologizing. You haven't done anything wrong."

"Sorry." I wince. "Bollocks, I keep saying that."

"Do all Brits apologize constantly?"

I eat another mac-and-cheese ball as an excuse not to speak for a moment. "Yes, we do apologize often. But saying 'sorry' doesn't always mean a person is expressing regret. It's sort of a national tic."

"Really?"

"Well, more so for me than everyone else."

"You don't need to be nervous with me." She slants forward a touch and speaks in a huskier voice. "As long as I live, I will never forget even one second of our time in that car. When you said you had an unusual idea, I never could've guessed what you had in mind." She sits back and fans herself with one hand. "All I can say is wow, you are an amazing lover."

Amazing? Me? She must have confused me with some other bloke who shagged her in a car. But no, I can't believe that. She might have gotten a leg over with a virtual stranger, but Rachelle doesn't seem like the casual-sex sort of woman.

"I had never tried that thing before," I tell her. "Saw it in a magazine once. Never imagined I'd have a reason to try it out. Honestly, I'm not as wonderful a lover as you seem to think. It was a one-off experience. A fluke, really."

She scoots her chair forward so she can reach across the table to clasp my hands. "You have some kind of complex about your sex appeal, don't you? Trust me, every woman who lays eyes on you wants to get in your pants."

Unfortunately, I had just taken a sip of brandy when she said that. Now, I splutter and spew the drink all over the table. "Bollocks. I'm so sorry, Rachelle. I'm not usually this clumsy, but then, I've never been so enamored of a woman before."

"You're enamored of me?"

I've finished wiping off the table, but I can't look at her. "You must know how I feel about you. It's obvious to everyone."

"Not to me." She studies me for a moment, though I can see her only peripherally. Then she pushes her chair back and walks around the table to kneel beside me. "I can't know for sure how you feel unless you talk to me about it. I like you, Kendall, and I traveled all this way to find out if we could be more than casual lovers. Do you want to find out too?"

"Of course I do."

"Then we need to have real, honest conversations." She lays a hand on my thigh. "Can you do that without getting anxious?"

"I'll try. That's all I can reasonably promise."

Rachelle rises and flaps her hand in a get-up gesture. "Come on, we need to go outside and get away from any prying eyes, even if they are well-meaning."

I push my chair back and stand up, then face her. "Yes, let's take a walk through the garden. It's lovely and secluded."

"Sounds perfect."

We walk side by side as we exit the solarium, and I open the patio door for her, but we don't hold hands. I want to do that. It seems inappropriate, though, considering my behavior thus far. A man of my age should not become so enamored of a beautiful woman that he can't speak a coherent sentence, yet Rachelle does affect me that way. Her voice tickles my senses, and her smile gives me a pang in my chest. I do not believe in love at first sight. But clearly, I do subscribe to the idea of lust at first sight.

I suppose my behavior four months ago is responsible for my flustered behavior today. I still can't reconcile what we did in that car with the way I've behaved for most of my adult life. I'm a ruddy butler. Men like me do not shag strangers on bench seats while a driver is listening.

As we round the corner of the house, heading for the garden, Rachelle tentatively slips her fingers between mine. I curl my fingers round hers too, just as awkwardly. Then I glance at her precisely when she glances at me. We both blush this time. Yet we keep our fingers twined.

"What is your name?" she asks. "I still don't know."

"Yes, you do. My name is Kendall."

"I meant your whole name. First, middle, and last. I am Rachelle Marie Buckholtz."

"My name is Kendall. That's all."

"What, like Madonna or Bono?"

I do not want to give her the information she's trying to wheedle out of me. I should release her hand, but I can't do it. Her palm feels warm and soft and wonderful pressed to mine. Well, perhaps I do want to share my full name with her, but that never ends well which is precisely why I never speak those words.

Rachelle bumps her shoulder into my upper arm. "Don't be shy. I won't tell anybody I know your full name, and I'm really good at keeping secrets."

"It's rather embarrassing."

That's an understatement, and I don't care to test her affection for me, not this early in our acquaintance. Perhaps I will never share the information with her.

Rachelle snuggles up to me, wrapping both her arms round my bicep. She rests her chin on my arm too, even while we continue ambling toward the garden. "Please, Kendall. Please, please, please, tell me your full name. I told you mine. Buckholtz isn't exactly a sexy surname."

"It's nothing compared to my full name." I suddenly realize that I might be going about this the wrong way. I need to distract her from asking me that question again. "I've never met any women called Rachelle. Is that a French name?"

"Yes. I'm impressed you know that. My mom is a native Frenchwoman, but she moved to America to go to college, and that's where she met my dad, who's American."

"Are your parents still together?"

"No. They got divorced during my junior year of college. Mom wanted to move back to France, but Dad refused to do that. He had a business he'd spent years building up, and he didn't want to throw that away. Mom runs an online business, which means she could do that anywhere."

"Was the divorce mutually agreed on?"

She grins. "I love the way you talk, and I don't mean just your accent. You sound like a sexy Victorian, hot in bed but stuffy the rest of the time. It's cute."

"But you have never been in bed with me. We shagged in the backseat of a Mercedes."

"You know what I meant."

We've just reached the entrance to the garden, so I stop us there and turn toward her. "I won't tell you my full name. Either accept that or our acquaintance will end."

She folds her arms under her breasts, lifting them just enough to distract me briefly. "What's the big secret? Are you a mafia enforcer?"

"I have never been a mafioso. And I doubt you believe that, anyway."

"No, you don't seem like the type. But you're being awfully cagey for a man who claims to be just a butler." Rachelle tips her head to the side and squints at me as if she's analyzing me. "Do the Parrishes know your top-secret name?"

"Only the Dowager Lady Sommerleigh knows my secrets."

"Rosalyn? She knows?" Rachelle leans toward me. "You just admitted you have more than one secret. Are you or have you ever been a covert operative?"

A bark of laughter spurts out of me, but it's a bit nervous. "Do I seem like a ruddy spy? No, I have never been a covert operative. Are you done interrogating me now?"

"Not even close. But I can wait for those answers."

"Thank you."

She wags a finger at me. "Don't think you're completely off the hook. Real conversation means talking about our pasts."

"I will tell you what I'm comfortable sharing. Once we know each other better..." I scratch my cheek and shrug. "Perhaps I'll feel safe telling you the rest."

"That still sounds like you're on the lam from bad people."

Of course she thinks that. I don't blame her. Somehow, I need to explain without sharing the details. So, I lead Rachelle into the garden and gesture for her to sit down on a concrete bench that lies deeper within the maze-like garden. She settles onto the bench, glancing left and right at the two birdbaths that flank it.

I sit down beside her, leaving a discreet distance between us. "I am not a criminal or an evil mastermind. But I have reasons for not wanting to reveal the details of my past."

"Okay, I get that. But can't you give me a crumb?"

"Yes, I think I can." I shift about and avoid looking directly at her. But that's rubbish. I need to look at her—so I do. "The elder Lord Sommerleigh hired me when I was twenty-six and Hugh was only twelve. Rosalyn, Lady Sommerleigh, kept me on after Lawrence passed away."

"You've known Hugh since he was twelve? Wow, you don't look old enough to have been an adult back then."

"People often comment on that. The elder Lord and Lady Sommerleigh took an enormous chance when they hired me, since my previous career had been, ah, less than admirable."

Rachelle's brows rise.

"Nothing criminal," I assure her. "Only the Dowager Lady Sommerleigh knows about my past, and she has kept the secret for all these years."

"That must mean she trusts you."

"Yes. I would never do anything to embarrass the Parrishes, not willingly. Their devotion to me is reciprocated. I love them as if they were my own family."

"I admire that." She scoots a bit closer to me. "Do you get along with your parents?"

"Yes, as long as we don't discuss my former career. They disapproved and felt humiliated by what I'd done. Still, I send money to Mum and Dad on a monthly basis." I bow my head to stare down at the earth beneath my feet. "I'm a coward. I've been hiding out at Sommerleigh ever since."

"Oh, I doubt you're a coward. Whatever your secret is, once you tell me about it, you'll feel much better." She squeezes my thigh gently. "I can wait until you're ready to open up."

And I desperately want to tell her everything. But I've been down that road before, and it always ended in disaster. Might Rachelle be different? I hope that's the case, yet I need more than a few hours with her to determine if she is the one woman who will understand my past.

Could I be that lucky? Only time will tell.

Chapter Five

Rachelle

Kendall and I wander through the gorgeous gardens of Sommerleigh in a companionable silence. We smile at each other often and hold hands the whole time. When I ask about the types of flowers, trees, and shrubs on the estate, Kendall lights up as he explains them all to me. I'm amazed that a butler knows so much about gardens, but I guess I shouldn't be surprised. He told me he's lived at Sommerleigh for a long time. It's essentially his home.

Well-manicured hedges define the garden and its multiple sections, rising high enough above our heads to provide privacy. They're basically green walls composed of tightly woven shrubs. But each section of the Sommerleigh garden offers different kinds of plants—hollyhocks, delphiniums, rambling roses, geraniums, wisteria, and more.

"How long has this garden been around?" I ask. "Seems like it must have taken decades to create it."

"Yes, it took many years. And the original Sommerleigh garden was much smaller. Lord Sommerleigh's great-great grandfather, Aldus Parrish, expanded and enhanced the garden as a wedding gift to his new bride."

I love how animated Kendall gets when he talks about hedges and flowers, but hearing the romantic tale about Hugh's great-great grandfather makes me wonder about something. "Have you ever been married, Kendall?"

"No. Have you?"

I shake my head. "Dating hasn't been a great experience for me. Most men just want to talk about themselves, and one guy actually told me that he was afraid I'd accuse him of sexual harassment. I can't believe you would ever feel that way."

"But I refuse to tell you about my past. Isn't that worse?"

"Not in my book. You're polite and chivalrous, two things that are rare these days." I wander over to a trellis that has pink hollyhocks wound around it and finger the blossoms. "I was engaged once, but it didn't work out."

Kendall comes up beside me. "Why not? You are a lovely, intelligent woman."

"My former fiancé would disagree."

"May I ask why? Sorry. That's none of my concern."

"Of course it's your concern." I clasp his hand, turning toward him. "We're dating, right? That means we should talk about stuff like that."

"Even though I won't discuss my past at all?"

"You have your reasons, I'm sure. But since this is just the beginning, I can wait to learn more about you." I sigh as I remember my previous relationship. "Tim didn't have much interest in sex, and when we made love, it was strictly missionary with no foreplay."

Oh, shit. Why did I blurt that out?

Kendall's eyes go wide as he stops blinking. For a moment, he says nothing, though he stares into my eyes. I think I spot a slight blush firing up on his cheeks too, but then it fades away before I can be sure.

He clears his throat and straightens his tie. The butler wears a three-piece suit, and it looks damn sexy on him. "I'm sorry to hear that. You are such a passionate woman that I find it hard to believe you could become engaged to a man like that."

"Well, he was a nice guy. He just had no interest in getting more adventurous in the bedroom, and I never bothered to suggest doing anything outdoors or even in a different room in our house. I knew he'd balk."

"I used to believe in only bog-standard sex. But then, ah, an event changed my mind." He glances at me sideways, making the cutest shy expression. "You were that event."

"You suddenly became awesome at sex?"

"No. I suddenly realized I wanted more than the bog-standard variety."

I laugh just a little, purely because the way he talks is adorable. "The term bog-standard must be a British thing, hey? I like it. You Brits are so creative with your slang."

"Well, I can't speak to that. But 'bog-standard' means that something is utterly ordinary." He smiles again in that sweetly shy way. "I haven't enjoyed a good chin wag in ages."

"And that means…"

"I love chatting with you."

"Yeah, I figured that's what it meant, but there was a chance it means something completely weird in British."

"We don't have our own language. We speak English." He glances at his watch. "I need to get back to my job."

"Of course. I can hang out with the Parrishes."

We wend our way through the garden, returning to the spot where we'd begun, and he holds my hand until we reach the exit. I'm somewhat disappointed when he lets go, but I realize he has a job to do and it requires the utmost decorum. He believes that. I doubt the Parrishes give a hoot if Kendall puts a fork in the wrong place on the dinner table or if his tie gets a teeny bit askew.

He escorts me to the sitting room, where the Parrishes are waiting. Kendall ushers me over to a chair by the fireplace, where a small fire burns, just enough to keep the room a comfortably lukewarm temperature. Once I've sat down, he bows and turns to leave.

"Wait, Kendall," Hugh says. "You're allowed to take the day off. In fact, we have all agreed that you need more than a day's relaxation. How would you like to take a three-week holiday?"

"I'd rather not, sir. I prefer to do my job."

"But Rachelle is here."

Rosalyn rises and walks over to Kendall, touching his arm. "Come now, pet, you don't honestly prefer to work when you could be enjoying time with Rachelle. Do you?"

"I don't wish to offend you, but I do indeed prefer to remain at my post."

She studies him for a moment with her lips clamped together. Then she exhales a long sigh. "All right, Kendall, as you wish."

He hurries out of the sitting room.

Then Hugh and Avery rise from the sofa, stretching and yawning in the most contrived way. Lord Sommerleigh says, "I don't know about you, darling, but I could use a lie-down."

"Oh, me too. What about you, Rosalyn?"

"I am not in the least tired."

Hugh stretches again, yawning even more loudly. "Have it your way, Mum. We're off to bed."

As soon as the door shuts behind Hugh and Avery, Rosalyn moves onto the sofa and pats the opposite end. "Come sit with me, dear. We need to have a conversation."

I shuffle over to the sofa and sit down. "A conversation about what?"

"Kendall, of course."

"Not sure he would appreciate me gossiping about him."

Rosalyn shakes her head, giving me a motherly smile. "No need for gossip, dear. This will be an entirely factual discussion."

"About Kendall. Shouldn't you talk to him if you're going to discuss him?"

"The lovely boy won't listen, believe me. But you and I can figure things out together."

Not sure I like the sound of that. Rosalyn seems like a nice lady, but honestly, I don't know her. And I've gotten the distinct impression that Kendall treasures his privacy. But I am curious about what the Dowager Lady Sommerleigh wants to discuss. "We can talk about Kendall, but you shouldn't tell me anything that he wouldn't want anyone else to know about him."

Rosalyn smiles knowingly. "I was right about you. The moment we met, I knew you would be the only woman who could get under his skin and make him want to do something other than fetching drinks and snacks for us."

"Is that really all he does at Sommerleigh? I know he's a butler, but I don't understand the scope of his job."

"His duties are diverse, and over the years, he has become a sort of manager for the household. Frankly, we couldn't do without him." She angles toward me and clasps her hands on her lap. "Has Kendall told you how he came to live here with us?"

"He said your husband hired him, and that he spent a lot of time with Hugh who was only a boy back then."

"That is true. Kendall is like a son to me."

"Is he young enough to be your son?" The second I spoke those words, I realized I shouldn't have asked the question. Kendall should tell me the answer himself, in his own time. "I'm sorry. That was inappropriate."

"Not at all. Your curiosity is understandable."

I did not overlook the fact that she didn't answer my question, but I can let that go for now. Kendall should be the one to tell me, not Rosalyn. So, I switch gears with the conversation. "I heard that your son used to be very popular with the ladies."

She smiles with a twinkle in her eyes. "You are quite diplomatic. I appreciate that, but it's unnecessary. Everyone knows that my son used to be a ladies' man, to put it mildly. He has always treated women with respect, but he was very popular. He slept with more women than I would care to recall, but his behavior in Scotland last year finally forced him to take a hard look at himself in the mirror."

"That sounds like a great story."

"Oh, yes, it was. Hugh nearly lost his best mate, Callum MacTaggart, in the process. It took a small army of Scots, Brits, and Americans to shake sense into him." Her smile slants upward at one corner. "That experience prepared Hugh so that he wouldn't cock it up when he finally met the right woman—Avery Hahn. I adore my daughter-in-law."

"Did Kendall sort of raise Hugh?"

"Yes, I suppose you could say that. Kendall treated Hugh like a younger brother, though I could tell he didn't approve of Hugh's behavior after he became the Viscount Sommerleigh. I didn't approve either, but Kendall and I never discussed my son's fall from grace."

I feel like I've been transported into a TV soap opera. My life before I met Kendall had been dull by comparison, and I guess I'm a little bit starstruck by the way my life has changed. Hunting down Kendall brought me to these wonderful, strange people who make me feel like they've known me forever.

Someone raps on the door three times, discreetly.

Rosalyn sighs as her lips curl up a touch. "That would be Kendall. The dear boy always knocks three times. The rest of the staff don't bother to announce themselves at all. They simply walk into the room—as long as it's a public space like the sitting room. Lawrence and I always encouraged our staff to think of Sommerleigh as their home."

The more I learn about these people, the more I love them.

"Come in, Kendall," Rosalyn calls out. "Don't be shy, dear. Rachelle won't ravish you in my presence."

She winks at me.

No idea what that's supposed to mean. But since I met this woman, I've realized she has an impish sense of humor.

The door inches open, and Kendall pokes his head through the gap. "Ma'am, may I enter the sitting room?"

"Yes, you silly boy, I already gave you an invitation."

Kendall straightens and walks over to us, his expression unreadable. He hands Rosalyn an envelope. "Lord Sommerleigh instructed me to deliver this to you."

"Thank you, dear." She waves toward a chair. "Sit down, Kendall. I enjoy admiring attractive younger men, but not when they stand there like a granite statue. Sit down and relax. Please."

He settles his butt onto a chair but remains perched on its edge while retaining his perfect posture.

Rosalyn gives him an affectionate, if exasperated, look. Then she rips the envelope open. After reading whatever is inside it, she compresses her lips as if she's trying not to smile and slips the note back into the envelope.

"Everything okay?" I ask.

"Oh, yes, pet. Everything is just fine." She tucks the envelope into her skirt pocket. "My son requires my assistance with a certain matter. Kendall, I command you to attend to Rachelle's every need until I return. I shall meet you both in the dining room at seven o'clock."

Kendall's eyes widen, though only for a second or two. Then he clears his throat and regains his composure. "But, ma'am, I have duties—"

"Do as you're told. Please."

"Of course, ma'am."

Rosalyn stands up, sweeps her gaze over me and Kendall in turn, then strides out the door. As it clicks shut behind her, Kendall furtively glances at me.

"What should we do now?" I ask. "Rosalyn ordered us to… Well, I'm actually not sure what she thinks we should be doing."

"Neither do I."

I drum my fingers on my knees.

He fiddles with his tie.

Birds chirp outside the window.

Finally, I can't stand it any longer. "This is ridiculous. We've had sex, for heaven's sake. It shouldn't be hard for us to talk to each other. I mean, we did that out in the garden, but suddenly, it's awkward."

"My fault, I'm sure."

"There's no blame on either side. Rosalyn left us here, hoping that something would happen. No idea what that something is."

He gazes at me steadily for a moment. "Would you care for a drink?"

"Sure. But nothing alcoholic." Is he trying to get away from me? That doesn't really seem likely, not after our discussion in the garden.

Kendall rises and walks over to a large cabinet. I had noticed that cabinet before but didn't know what it held. Now, he swings the halves of the doors open to reveal the bottles and glasses that had been hidden within the cabinet, which stands a foot higher than Kendall's head. The base is about six inches off the floor, but from there up the cabinet is filled with all sorts of bottles—wine, champagne, whiskey, and other things I don't recognize.

He plucks two bottles from a lower shelf and twists the caps off them. The clear glass allows the color of the reddish-brown liquid to show.

"What is that?" I ask. "Never seen anything like it. The liquid is such a beautiful shade."

Kendall saunters over to the sofa and drops onto it while still holding the two bottles. "Would you like to come over here? Or should I bring your bottle to you?"

"I'd love to join you over there."

He watches while I get up and amble over to the sofa. When I take a seat beside him, he doesn't seem at all surprised. He hands me a bottle. "This is dandelion and burdock, a nonalcoholic beverage that's popular here in the UK and in Ireland as well, I believe. I've never visited Ireland, so I can't state that with certainty."

I take a sip of the drink. "Mm, I like it. What's in this stuff?"

"Fermented dandelion and burdock roots." He sips from his bottle several times while watching me enjoy the drink. His lips kink up into the cutest little smile. "I'm glad the Dowager Lady Sommerleigh encouraged us to spend more time alone, but I suspect she and Lord Sommerleigh are up to something."

"Poppy mentioned to me that she and her friends are part of the American Wives Club and that the whole purpose of the club is to meddle in other people's lives."

"Yes, that's true." He takes a large swig of his drink. "I suspect they're plotting to meddle in our lives."

"Me and you? We barely know each other. It's way too soon for anyone to butt their noses into our relationship. We don't really have a relationship yet, anyway. It's barely a bud of something, nowhere near a bloom."

But yeah, I think I'd love for that bud to blossom.

Chapter Six

Kendall

I appreciate your gardening metaphor, Rachelle. But alas, I have seen what the American Wives Club can and does do in the name of love." I glance down at the clear bottle in my hand, which now is half empty. "Think I need a stronger beverage if we are meant to be the club's next victims."

"Did that group play a role in Hugh's transformation?"

"A role?" I can't help laughing just a little. "No, they abducted him and held him hostage in a medieval castle until he agreed to do what the club members believed was best. They did the same for Callum MacTaggart and Kate Wagner, though Kate was never abducted or held captive."

Though I wasn't there for the festivities in Scotland, I heard all the details when the Parrishes came home. I wasn't a party to the discussions, but in my role as butler I couldn't help overhearing. Hugh had been devastated when he lost Kate Wagner to Callum MacTaggart and no longer wanted to be a ladies' man. Yes, I can say that the club's meddling helped Hugh. But I am not and never have been a womanizer. That means I do not need anyone to interfere in my life.

Rachelle takes a few slow sips of her drink while she considers me. "The steamrolling worked, right? Hugh and Callum are both happily married, and they're best friends again."

As I sink back into the sofa, I can't help eying her with a touch of suspicion. "I hope you aren't suggesting that we should surrender to the meddling."

"Do you think all those people mean well and want to help you?"

"Of course they mean well. But having good intentions doesn't negate the fact that they don't need to 'help' me." I guzzle the remainder of my dandelion and burdock, then wipe my mouth with the back of my hand. "They can't meddle when they know so little about me. I'm virtually a stranger to them."

"But Rosalyn and Hugh have known you for a long time. They must have learned a few things about you over the years. Besides, Rosalyn admitted to me that she knows all about your mysterious background."

I can't deny that, and though I prefer not to reveal that information yet, I do feel I owe her some sort of explanation. "Yes, the elder Lord and Lady Sommerleigh both knew about my background, including my former occupation and my family. But they never met my parents."

"Are your mom and dad horrible people?"

"No. They couldn't accept what I did for a living, that's all." I sink deeper into the sofa, slouching so low that my head lies at the level of her tits. "It's my fault. I should have searched harder for a different job instead of taking the easy way out. Mum and Dad are decent, hard-working people who would never speak an unkind word."

But that's all I can tell her right now. After what I endured when everyone who had known me back then found out about my career, I simply can't risk sharing any of that with Rachelle until we know each other better. Honestly, I'd rather not share that with her at all. If we grow closer... I shouldn't worry about that yet. It's too soon.

Fortunately, Rachelle changes the subject. "How crazy do these friends of yours get with their meddling?"

"I have not been the object of their interference, but the blokes who are married to women in the American Wives Club abducted Lord Sommerleigh last year."

"Abducted him? Where did they take Hugh?"

"To Scotland. I sort of skipped over that part when I discussed the situation involving Callum MacTaggart and Lord Sommerleigh. Not intentionally." I push a hand into my hair and shut my eyes. "It's all been rather a whirlwind since you came back into my life."

"For me too. But I can't picture any of those people doing insane things like that on behalf of you and me."

"You don't know them the way I do."

I can hear her breathing and tapping a fingernail on her bottle of dandelion and burdock. For a moment or two, I allow myself to enjoy listening to those little sounds and the knowledge that she's there beside me. I haven't felt this comfortable with anyone, especially a woman, in so long that I can't even count the span of time. More than anything, I want to get to know her and vice versa. But that won't happen overnight.

Slowly, I turn my head toward her and open my eyes. "Would you like to date me?"

Rachelle freezes with her lips wrapped around the rim of her bottle. She rotates her eyes toward me. "Date? Do you mean, like, dinner and a movie?"

"Whatever you prefer. I want us to become better acquainted. That's the traditional way of determining if we are indeed compatible."

"I'd like that." She sets her bottle down on the coffee table and leans toward me to kiss my cheek. "I would love to date you, Kendall."

To hear her declare that, it makes me want to jump up and down whilst shouting with joy. That's a ridiculous idea. Yet I can't help feeling this way. The thought of dating Rachelle Buckholtz makes me feel…giddy. I'm too bloody old to behave that way, so I'll keep it to myself.

Rachelle turns her entire body toward me, tucking her legs beneath her. "So, now that we're dating, will you at least tell me your full name?"

"Not yet."

"Are you afraid I'll spill the beans to the whole world? I would never do that to you."

"I know. But my full name is…unusual. Revolting might be a better description."

She pulls her chin back. "Revolting? Oh, now you absolutely have to tell me. Buckholtz isn't exactly a sexy surname, you know. But I still told it to you."

"Your surname is charming compared to mine."

"Hmm. I think you have a complex about your full name, but I can wait until you're ready to share it. Maybe I can even convince you not to keep it a secret." She raises a hand when I begin to speak. "No more pestering you about your name, I promise. But I don't even know how old you are. It's kind of weird."

Perhaps if I give her one snippet of information, she will relent for a while. "I am forty-three years old."

"Seriously? You look like you're in your twenties."

"Yes, I've been told as much before." I eye her sideways. "How old are you?"

"Thirty-nine."

I scrutinize her with exaggerated care, squinting my eyes and puckering my lips. "Thirty-nine, eh? I would've thought you're forty-nine."

She snatches up a throw pillow and tosses it at my head. "Very funny. You really don't want to ever get laid again, do you?"

"Was that meant to be a threat? Because I had no trouble talking you into shagging me in the backseat of Lord Sommerleigh's Mercedes five minutes after we met."

I toss that pillow back at her.

She picks it up again and wields it as if she means to strike me, but I snatch the pillow away from her, flinging it across the room. I wrap my arms around Rachelle and drag her down onto the sofa so I can flip us both over, which means I now lie stretched out on top of her body. When I pin her wrists to the sofa's arm, she licks her lips and then rubs them together.

"What are you doing, Kendall? I mean, it's not like you would ever screw me in the sitting room. Anybody might walk in here."

"You have recurrent amnesia concerning our time in the Mercedes, don't you?"

She shakes her head. "I remember every second of it. Now, if you want to do that unusual thing again, right here in the sitting room, I'm totally on board for that."

"Are you?" I push my leg between her thighs and rub my knee into her groin, making her suck in a sharp breath. "That particular thing isn't the only unusual option I know of."

"Show me another one. Please."

I shift my other leg as I attempt to get into a different position, but I lose my balance and tumble off the sofa. When I thump down onto the floor, I bump my head on the coffee table. "Bollocks!"

Rachelle springs upright, eyes wide. "Kendall! Are you okay?"

"Fine, yes. It was a slight bump, that's all." I sit up and palpate the back of my head. "That wasn't too clever, was it? I'm no gymnast."

"Yeah, you didn't quite stick the landing." She slides onto the floor, kneeling in front of me, and brushes her fingers through my hair. "I like that you're kind of clumsy sometimes. It makes you more human."

"So, being an utter klutz is the benchmark? Wish I'd known that years ago. It would have made dating much easier."

The sitting room door flies open.

We both turn our attention in that direction.

Lord and Lady Sommerleigh have both thrust their heads into the narrow gap between the door and the jamb. They grin at us like children who know a secret and can't wait to tell their parents.

Hugh pushes the door open all the way. "May we come in? You could say no, but this is my house."

Avery elbows him in the side. "Our house."

"Of course, darling. Sometimes I forget that we're married, simply because I'm so overjoyed to have you for my bride."

"You are so full of shit, Hugh."

"Of course I am. But you love that about me."

They both seem to abruptly notice that I'm sitting on the floor with Rachelle beside me. Lord and Lady Sommerleigh exchange confused glances. Then Hugh clears his throat. "Mind getting up off the floor, mate? It's rather strange to have a conversation this way."

I clamber to my feet and help Rachelle up too.

Hugh and Avery approach us, exchanging another glance that I can't interpret. Then Hugh speaks. "We have made a unilateral decision about your immediate future, Kendall."

"What? If you're sacking me—"

"Calm down," Hugh says with an accompanying hand gesture. "No one is being sacked. This decision is a positive change."

I dislike change of any sort. But he is my employer, and I must do what he wishes. So, I wait for his pronouncement.

Hugh leans forward slightly and smiles in his mischievous way. "We're sending you away on a three-week holiday."

"But I don't want a holiday, sir. I prefer to remain at Sommerleigh."

"What you mean is that you'd rather keep hiding out here." Hugh rests an arm across Avery's shoulders. "The time has come for our little bird to learn to fly on his own."

"I don't understand."

"This is for your own good," Avery says. "You and Rachelle need more time to get acquainted, and you can't do that properly while you're at Sommerleigh House."

Hugh gazes lovingly at his wife. "Sometimes a man needs to shake up his life before he can appreciate what's right in front of him."

Avery kisses his cheek.

Hugh faces me again. "This is not a request, Kendall. It is, in fact, a command from Lord and Lady Sommerleigh. You and Rachelle will take the next three weeks to get better acquainted. Your holiday begins..." He checks his watch. "Well, technically, it began three and a half minutes ago. But I digress. The point is that you may not return to Sommerleigh until seven p.m. on October 31."

"But, sir, I don't want to leave. Rachelle and I can get acquainted here at home."

He wags a finger at me. "No, no, no, Kendall. That won't do. Must I invoke the power of my title to convince you? Alternately, I could bring in Dominic and Derek to kidnap you the way the American Wives Club did to me."

"No, sir, I do not wish to be abducted."

"Then you have just one option. Give in, mate. Leave the nest and spread your wings."

If he makes another bird metaphor, I might whack him with the lamp on the end table. "I am older than you, Lord Sommerleigh. You can't order me to do anything."

"Ah, but I am your employer as well as your friend. That gives me all the power I need to boot you out of the house."

"I don't have a car. You shouldn't make Arthur serve as our driver on this bloody annoying forced holiday."

Hugh chuckles. "Oh, no, we need Arthur here at home. I've arranged alternate transportation for you and Rachelle. I happen to know you have a driving license, Kendall."

"Yes, but I don't own a car."

Lord Sommerleigh smirks, then digs about in his trouser pocket until he produces a set of car keys. "Here you are."

He tosses the keys to me.

I catch them and stare blankly at the tag. "You're lending me your Jaguar?"

"Yes."

"But you won't even let your best mate drive it."

Hugh chuckles again. "That's because Callum is a maniac on four wheels. I might trust him to drive me somewhere on his Harley, but not in his car. You, on the other hand, are a responsible bloke."

"Thank you, sir, but—"

"Oh, I almost forgot." Hugh digs about in his other trouser pocket and produces another item. "This is for you too."

He tosses me the keys. "What is this for?"

"My flat in London. You and Rachelle will stay there for the duration. The flat does have a guest room if she prefers to sleep alone."

I stare down at the two sets of keys in my hand. Lord Sommerleigh is lending me his car and his flat. Either he wants me out of his hair because he's tired of me, or he wants me gone because he genuinely believes Rachelle might be the right woman for me. I had never known Hugh to meddle in other people's lives until after he met Avery. Now, he seems incapable of not meddling.

But he and Avery are doing this for *me*.

"Don't look so stunned," Hugh says as he claps a hand on my shoulder. "You are family, after all. Lawrence Parrish was a wonderful father, but you are the one who secretly taught me how to play poker and how to win a girl over. I became a ladies' man because of you."

"That is not a compliment, Hugh."

He freezes, drawing his head back slightly. "Did uptight Kendall just call me by my first name? It's a miracle."

"Well, ah... Sorry, sir."

"One day, you will gladly call me Hugh. I can wait for that." He slants toward me and speaks softly. "You didn't make me a manwhore, to use the word my wife prefers, but you showed me how a real man treats a woman. I'm sorry I wasted that wisdom for so many years. I hope you can forgive me for that."

"There's nothing to forgive. I understand why you fell apart after Lawrence passed away, and I'm proud of the man you've become."

Are his eyes tearing up? Hugh shuffles backward a few steps and sniffles while keeping his head bowed. When he looks at me again, his smile is like none I've ever seen before. "You are my brother, Kendall. In spirit if not in blood."

I can't think of a ruddy thing to say in response. But I don't need to speak, do I? Hugh knows exactly what his family has meant to me.

Hugh claps a hand down on my shoulder once again. "Go find your bliss, mate. You deserve it."

Chapter Seven

Rachelle

Kendall seems genuinely surprised by everything Hugh told him. I don't think he realized that the Parrishes consider him to be part of their family, but I could see that the moment I met them. Whatever Kendall's dirty little secrets are, I doubt the Parrishes will care about that when he finally tells them. They're good people. I fell in love with them immediately.

"Go on," Hugh says to Kendall. "Take your girl and have a bloody good time playing silly buggers for three weeks."

"Silly buggers?" I say. "Somebody needs to give me a dictionary of British slang."

"No, pet, you have a walking dictionary standing right beside you." He nods toward Kendall. "Let him induct you into our world."

There's no one else I'd rather do that with, and I'm not even making a sexual innuendo. Spending time with Kendall sounds like the best vacation ever.

Hugh and Avery escort us through the house, but on our way to the front door, we bump into Rosalyn. She beams at me and Kendall as we walk down the hallway, clearly thrilled that Kendall and I are going away together. But she stops us halfway to our destination.

"Rachelle, darling, I fell in love with you the moment we met. And I can tell dear Kendall feels the same way." She kisses my cheek. "Help the sweet boy loosen up a bit, would you?"

I salute her. "Yes, ma'am, I will fulfill your orders."

Rosalyn lays a hand on my cheek and another on Kendall's, beaming again as she looks at us both.

"Hurry it up, Lord Sticky!" someone shouts from further down the hall. "We're all waiting."

Lord Sommerleigh rolls his eyes. "Piss off, Dominic! We'll get there when we get there, you cheeky sod." Then he reverts to his normal voice, no longer shouting. "Dom has adopted the nickname created by my brother-in-law. I will never forgive Derek for speaking that phrase in front of my mates."

We finally reach the foyer, where Dominic and Chelsea wait for us. Four other people wait there as well, and I recognize all but two. The driver, Arthur, as well as the maid, Beatrice.

Rosalyn gestures toward the foursome. "Rachelle, I believe you've met Arthur and Beatrice. Now, may I introduce you to our cook, Mildred, and Simon, the best horticulturist in the UK if not the world. He is responsible for the voluptuous garden here at Sommerleigh."

Next, Kendall and I say goodbye to his friends. Each of them, including the servants, approaches to shake Kendall's hand and kiss my cheek. They all seem genuinely thrilled that the butler is finally taking a well-deserved holiday. I didn't come up with that phrase. They did. Each and every person, including the Parrishes as well as Dominic and Chelsea, pronounces that Kendall is the keystone of this household and that they love him for everything he does and for who he is.

I don't think he ever realized how much everyone appreciates and relies on him. That makes me want to know more about him.

After the goodbyes are over, Kendall clasps my hand and leads me out to the driveway. The pea gravel crunches under our feet. He opens the front passenger door of the four-door Jaguar for me, even offering me his hand to help me get into the vehicle. Once he has shut the door, he starts walking around to the other side.

But Hugh jogs up to him and snatches the keys away just long enough to click a button. The trunk pops open. I can't hear what they're saying, but Kendall seems mildly surprised. Hugh returns the keys to him and says something that makes Kendall avert his gaze.

That's embarrassment. I've seen that a lot from him.

Kendall shuts the trunk and climbs into the driver's seat.

"What was Hugh showing you?" I ask. "Stolen goods?"

"No. He showed me our luggage."

"I don't understand. My luggage is at my hotel."

Kendall starts up the engine and gives me a long-suffering look. "You still haven't grasped the full extent of their meddling. They checked you out of your hotel and brought your things to Sommerleigh. That's why Dominic and Chelsea are here."

"Oh, I see. Wow, these people are unusually determined to mess around in our lives, aren't they?"

He grunts. "You have no idea."

I wriggle in my seat, strictly to get the full experience of sitting on a plush leather seat in a luxury car. "Ready to go? I'm excited to see Hugh's flat. It must be super-spiffy, huh?"

"Presumably. I've never been there." Kendall grips the steering wheel with both hands while staring straight out the windshield. "Are you sure you want to stay in Hugh's flat with me? I could drop you at a hotel instead."

Translation: *Rachelle, you can't possibly want to share an apartment with me, but I really, really want to screw you again, so please come with me to a fancy "flat."* Okay, he isn't that callous. But Kendall is oddly anxious about being with me. It must have something to do with his previous career, the one he won't talk about.

"I want to stay with you. If you'd rather I sleep in the spare room, I'm fine with that."

"We can discuss the specific arrangements once we get there."

"Good idea."

He starts up the engine but doesn't push the gas pedal. "Would you like to go somewhere else before we head to Hugh's flat? You haven't seen much of the city, I gather."

"No, not this time or the last time. Something personal came up four months ago, but I'm one hundred percent ready for sightseeing now."

Kendall nods, then starts driving.

I start to feel itchy, and I decide that means I should fess up about one thing. "Just so you know, I had to leave suddenly four months ago because my dad got in a car wreck and broke his leg. He needed months of physical therapy, but he's fine now. And he encouraged me to try to find you again."

"Then I owe him a debt of gratitude that I can never repay."

Neither of us speaks until we've left the Sommerleigh estate behind us and have started down the road. I'm pretty sure he'd be fine with driving for two and a half hours in silence, but I'm not.

"Do you have an idea for sightseeing?" I ask. "You must know all the best places."

"I'm not a tour guide. We need a map or something."

"Well, I have an idea. Not sure if you'll like it, though."

Kendall glances at me peripherally. "Tell me."

"Could we go to Poppy's bookshop?"

His brows hike up. "That's the first place you want to see?"

"It's where we met. I'd kind of like to revisit the shop that turned me into a lunatic who hunts down men she meets in bookshops."

"If you are a lunatic, so am I. But yes, we can go to Poppy's shop."

"Thank you. Mind if I turn on the radio?"

"It's Hugh's car. Do whatever you bloody well please." He slows down to turn a corner and takes the opportunity to slide a hand down my inner thigh. "Is it too soon for a shag? You've only been in the UK for two days."

Laughter splutters out of me. "Too soon? We had sex five minutes after we met, while in the backseat of Lord Sommerleigh's car with Arthur in the front."

"But we haven't sullied Lord Sommerleigh's Jaguar yet."

"Does anyone else ever get to see this side of you? I guess what I'm really asking is how often you date."

Kendall scrunches up his face. "Not often at all. I have never brought a woman back to Sommerleigh, and most of my dates involved a quick dinner and an even quicker shag."

"But you seem like the settling-down type."

"Women don't appreciate my former career or the fact that my parents are both factory workers."

"Sounds like you date obnoxious gold-diggers."

"I admit I haven't chosen my dates wisely." He pulls his hand away from my thigh. "After several women balked at my previous career, I was, ah, anxious about dipping my toes into those waters again."

"Afraid a shark might bite your toe off?"

"Something like that." He takes a deep breath and releases it slowly. The action seems to relax him. "But I don't feel that way with you. Any woman who would cross an ocean just to find me again can't be a gold-digging slag."

"Aw, shucks, what a sweet compliment." I smile and bat my eyelashes, just so he knows I'm kidding. "But seriously, I haven't had great luck with dating either. Men think it's weird that a single woman writes and illustrates children's books. Either that, or they decide I'm trying to rope them into marrying me on the first date."

"You create children's books?"

"That's right. Didn't I mention that before?"

He shakes his head. "I'm surprised you would feel comfortable talking about your life since I refuse to discuss mine."

"Let's make deal. For the rest of this trip, until we reach Poppy's bookshop, we won't talk about the past."

"You are far too kind, Rachelle, accepting that I don't want to explain my previous life to you. But yes, I would be happy to forget about all of that rubbish for now."

I kiss his cheek. "You really are the sweetest."

Are his cheeks turning faintly pink? Yep, they are. Every time I pay him a compliment, he does that.

"How about some music?" I say. "Not sure what UK radio has."

"You'll find our musical tastes are varied and not unlike those of Americans. We even have country and western stations."

"Seriously? I had no idea Brits liked that stuff."

"My father loves country music. Mum isn't a fan, so she didn't want to go line dancing with Dad. Instead, he took me with him, and that casual training paid off later."

"I won't ask why that is. Must have something to do with that period in your life that you aren't ready to talk about." I twist in my seat to get a better view of him. "Why did you confess that much? I didn't ask you to do it."

Kendall blushes again. "The words just came out. You make me feel so relaxed and comfortable that I might blurt out everything before the day is out."

Holy cow. I can't believe he not only spoke those words, but also seems totally unfazed by his confession. So, I cut him some slack and turn on the radio, then fuss with the dials until I find a pop station. I actually know most of these songs. *Huh.* I'd assumed British music would be alien to me. The up-tempo tunes inspire me to dance in my seat and sing along. Then Kendall joins in, and we're both belting out the cheesy, fun songs together. I love his voice when he's speaking, but to hear Kendall singing is an amazing experience. And strangely, it makes me horny.

We're traveling down a highway with few cars around us, and Kendall has just informed me that the highways all have M and A designations. I know he's trying to be a good tour guide, but I don't care about that right now. This inappropriate lust won't let go of me.

"Don't touch yourself that way unless you want me to fuck you, Rachelle."

"What way am I touching myself?"

He nods toward my lap. "You've been massaging your thighs while rocking your hips. And you also keep licking your lips every time you glance at me."

"What if I do want you to fuck me?"

"In the car?" His voice has dropped to a smoky timbre that makes me shiver with anticipation. "We shagged in the Mercedes, but we were passengers then. I'm driving right now."

"Can't help it. I want you now, Kendall."

He takes ragged breaths while twisting his hands around the steering wheel in slow, sensual movements. "I want you too, right now."

"Then let's do it."

"What precisely are you suggesting?"

I undo my seatbelt. "Sex in the car while we're roaring down the road."

"How will that work?"

"Just like this." I shimmy out of my panties, then climb over the center console to straddle his lap. "Get it now?"

"Yes, I understand. But it seems destined to result in a deadly car crash."

"Loosen up, Kendall. I've never done this before, but I know it'll work." I trace my fingers down his cheek and brush my lips over his. "So, the question is, do you trust me all the way?"

"I do."

"Then just keep your eye on the road and let me do the rest."

Kendall's lips tick up at the corners just enough that I know he genuinely wants to do this. When I begin to unbutton his vest, he starts to breathe more heavily. But he never looks away from the road, not even when I unhook his belt. Once I've unzipped his pants, I push a hand inside them to feel for his underpants.

"Holy shit, Kendall, I had no idea you were such a wild man in hiding."

"What? No one has ever called me that before."

"Oh, but you are wild." I clasp his cock with one hand. "A man who doesn't have any underwear on is definitely wild. What other secrets are you hiding underneath all that buttoned-up clothing?"

His lopsided smirk is the sexiest thing ever. "You've seen me completely starkers. I have no secrets from you—concerning my clothes, that is."

"I assume 'starkers' means naked."

"Yes."

While I position his dick at the lip of my opening, I keep glancing at his face to see his expression. "I love how hungry you look right now, and I'm so glad I wore a skirt today. Makes this much easier to accomplish."

He groans deeply as I sink down onto his lap, and I know he can feel every inch of me just like I feel every inch of him. "Fuck, Rachelle, I shouldn't want to do this in the car, but I do want that. Want it badly."

"Let me do all the work."

Kendall keeps both hands on the wheel while I set my hands on his shoulders and begin to ride him. I'm so wet that the friction of our bodies merging creates a liquid sucking sound that drives me to rock my hips faster and dig my nails into his shoulders. British pop music serves as the backdrop for our lovemaking, and I suddenly realize I'm riding him in time with the beats of the music. When a new song comes on, one with a driving and sensual tone, I can't stop myself from bouncing up and down on his cock while panting and letting out sharp little cries of desperation.

God, am I ever desperate—to feel him come inside me.

"Rachelle, ah, I need to thrust up into you. But that would be dangerous."

"Oh, Kendall, this feels so damn good."

His eyes widen and light up, while his lips curl into a deviously sexy smile. "I've just remembered something about this car."

"Huh?" I'm still riding him like a crazy cowgirl, so I can't understand what he just said.

Kendall does something on the steering wheel, pushing a button or whatever, then he splays his palms over my back and tugs me closer while he relaxes into his seat. "This is much better."

I freeze. "You need to drive the car."

"No, in point of fact, I do not."

Chapter Eight

Kendall

"What? Are you insane?" She doesn't try to climb off my lap or do anything to prevent us from crashing in a fiery blaze, as she clearly assumes will happen. "Kendall, a car can't drive itself."

"Of course it can. This Jaguar has driver assistance, which means it can keep the car in the correct lane and adjust the speed as necessary to ensure we stay on track."

"Never thought AI could be hot, but damn, I could kiss the computer in this car."

"I would prefer that you go on fucking me, not the computer."

"Me too."

I slide my hands round to her front so I can palm her breasts. Though I can't see them, I vividly remember what those luscious tits look like. "Go on, love, do whatever you like. The car will ensure we stay on the road."

She hesitates briefly, biting down on her bottom lip in a manner that makes me want to suck on that lip until it turns rosy red. But then she resumes riding me, and her excitement escalates even more swiftly now, as does mine. This woman is the most beautiful, incredible, sensual creature I've ever met. When I pinch her nipple lightly, she gasps and clenches my shirt with both hands. I massage her tits, my mouth watering at the prospect of tasting them.

Can't do that with our clothes on. Or can we?

She reaches down to tug on my sac, and the sensation makes me suck in a sharp breath. But when I fist my hand in her hair, yanking her head down to claim that sexy mouth, every last vestige of my common sense flies out of my brain.

I thrust my tongue deep and devour her with abandon.

Rachelle tears her mouth away from mine, breathing hard. "Need more leverage. Need it now."

"Yes, we do need that."

My mind has shifted into neutral, which means that my hormones are now in control. And they urge me to do something, anything, that will give us both what we crave. An orgasm. One so hard and hot that we might have an out-of-body experience.

Rachelle fumbles with one hand, trying to get hold of something beneath the seat, even while I consume her mouth yet again, thrusting my tongue wildly. She pauses in her mysterious task only long enough to tear her mouth away and say, "Oh, God, Kendall, the way you kiss me makes my clit pulsate and my nipples get so outrageously sensitive. I need you to make us both come."

"Can't do that. You're on my lap, love."

I grip her arse and thrust my other hand into her hair yet again, yanking her head down.

With her mouth millimeters from mine, she smiles with devious intent once again, then pulls on something.

I hear a click.

And the seat slams down into a nearly flat position.

She plants her palms on my chest, and with only the barest pause, begins fucking me in earnest. The seat creaks with every frenzied lunge of her hips.

If I had a vestige of common sense a moment ago, I now have none. She rides me so feverishly that her breaths turn into short, high-pitched squeaks. Even that noise turns me on more. I grasp the front of her blouse and rip it open. Tiny buttons go flying, but I don't give a toss about that. Relief rushes through me when I realize she's wearing a front-close bra, and all I need to do is tear those tiny clasps open. Then I latch my mouth onto her tit and suckle it hard.

She throws her head back and cries out.

I pick her up and drop her onto the backseat, then struggle to get out of the seat I'm lying on. She's already on her knees. Once I've crawled into position behind her, kneeling, I flip her so she's facing the rear window. "Hands on the glass. Now."

She slaps her palms on the window.

I kick her knees apart and grasp her hips, then plunge inside her sheath.

Her head falls backward, her hair tickling my lips.

I punch into her again and again, breathing so hard that my ears ring, and Rachelle cries out every time I sink my length deep inside her body, pounding into her like the wild man she called me moments ago. The windows have begun to fog up. Her palms drag across the glass every time I punch into her, creating clear trails on the window.

My cock throbs, and I know I need to make her come now.

I clasp one hand around her tit and rhythmically pinch that peak over and over, while at the same time I shove my other hand between her thighs to scrape my fingernail over her clit in an erratic rhythm.

Her body stiffens. Quick, strangled cries erupt out of her.

Then she comes.

I reposition my hand so the palm is rubbing her clit while I plunge three fingers inside her, ensuring she comes as hard as possible. Her body clenches my fingers again and again. Now that she has found her climax, I can't wait one second longer. I pull my hand away from her breast and clamp it onto her hip while I thrust several more times, unleashing everything I have inside her body. After two final thrusts, we're both done.

She sags against the backseat.

I sag against her, resting my chin on her shoulder. "Driver assistance is bloody wonderful."

Rachelle laughs. "Yeah, I'm kind of in love with it too."

We remain in the same position, with my cock still inside her, for a minute or so after we've finished. Then I realize one important fact. "Blimey. I need to get back in the driver's seat before we reach London. You should climb into your seat first."

She does that, then glances at me over the back of her seat, watching while I pull up my trousers. They had fallen down to my knees when I crawled into the back. I need to wriggle about until I at last accomplish my task and have my clothes in reasonable order again. Then I climb back into the driver's seat.

Rachelle holds onto the flaps of what had been her blouse. "You wrecked my shirt, Romeo."

"Yes, but our luggage is in the boot. We can stop at a petrol station so you can put on something more appropriate for public viewing." I rove my gaze over her bare breasts. "But it will be a shame to cover up those beautiful tits."

She tugs the halves of her blouse together. "It was worth the clothing damage to have a rockin' shag in Hugh's Jaguar."

"I love that you used the British term for fucking. You might become a native in no time."

"Don't hold your breath. I'm still an American girl, born and bred."

Twenty minutes later, we stop at a petrol station as I promised. Rachelle dashes into the loo with an undamaged blouse in her hand, returning with that garment now covering her torso. She climbs into the Jaguar and tosses her ruined blouse at me. It lands on my face.

"You broke it, you own it, Mr. No Last Name."

"For all you know, Kendall is my surname."

"True. But I also have some new theories about who you really are. Not just your name, but also your previous occupation."

I sigh heavily. "You won't give up on solving the mystery, will you? But I can promise that you will be disappointed when you learn the truth. It isn't as exciting as you hope."

Rachelle slants over the center console. "Well, if you told me your full name, I wouldn't need to come up with conspiracy theories about you."

"No conspiracies are involved. I am a dull, average man."

"Uh-huh." She sits back in her seat. "You'll never convince me that you're boring—now or in the past."

Fortunately, she gives up on interrogating me and resorts to dancing in her seat to the sugary pop music on the radio. She tries to sing along, but the songs aren't familiar to her, so she winds up inventing her own silly lyrics. They all revolve around me.

"I am not a ruddy piece of cake, Rachelle."

"Oh, yes, you are." She taps her fingers on the dashboard as if she's playing a piano and speaks in a singsong tone. "Kendall is mysterious, Kendall is so serious. The dirty butler, ooh, he's such a ruddy piece of sweet and steamy yumminess."

A laugh bursts out of me. "I'm beginning to rethink whether I want to spend the next three weeks with a barmy woman. A thirty-nine-year-old shouldn't behave like a randy teenager. And why did you use the word ruddy? Has meeting my friends addled your brain?"

She stops dancing in her seat and swivels her head to gawp at me.

"What's wrong now?" I ask. "Have you seen a ghost in the floorboard?"

"No, it's something much more shocking. You just called Hugh and the others your friends."

"Did I?"

She nods slowly. "You know what this means."

I'm fairly certain I don't want to hear what she believes it means. But I also realize that she will tell me anyway.

"Kendall, you are a part of the family. Not just the Parrish household, but Dominic and Chelsea and the others too."

I make a derisive noise. "I am the butler, nothing more."

"Bullshit. The only one you're fooling is yourself."

The hairs on my arms lift, and I experience a strange sensation that I think might be…happiness. I have lived with the Parrishes for a very long time, yet I never thought of them as mates. Certainly not as family. But they have been treating me differently of late, and they're determined to interfere in my life the way they often do with other people.

Blimey. They are my mates.

Rachelle goes back to singing with the radio while I focus on driving so I won't have to consider the ramifications of my epiphany. Because if those barmy people do think of me as family, then that means they will treat me like family too which means they mean to meddle in my life, and that means…I'm completely buggered.

The beautiful ginger-haired woman beside me settles down at last and relaxes into her seat. "How much longer until we get to London?"

"Not long."

"Do you realize that every time we're in a car together, we end up screwing each other's brains out in the backseat? Maybe we should start taking the bus."

"We'll need to come up with more inventive ways of shagging. But a bus is not on my bucket list."

"Not even if it's a red bus?"

"Hmm. Perhaps if we were on the top level… But no, we would end up sitting behind annoying teenagers who laugh too loudly."

"And we might get arrested." She turns the entire upper half of her body toward me. "I would love to do that unusual thing with you again sometime. We could be really crazy and do it in a bed this time."

"You are the only woman I have ever shagged in a car."

Rachelle lifts one leg to rest it on the center console. She had already removed her shoes earlier, so now she simply wriggles her toes to tickle my hand. She can't tickle my arms. I'm wearing my suit again.

"Kendall, why do you always wear a three-piece suit? I like it, but we're on vacation. You could, I don't know, try rolling up your sleeves. Or, you could go totally crazy and change into a T-shirt and jeans."

"I never dress that way. My job requires me to be professional."

"You really don't understand the concept of a vacation, do you?" She just tapped my hand with her big toe. Now, she unhooks her seatbelt so she can stretch out lengthwise across her seat and have better access to me for the sole purpose of teasing me mercilessly. She rubs the sole of her foot up and down my arm. "You would look so hot in a pair of swim briefs."

"It's my understanding a garment like that is skintight and barely covers a bloke's, ah, private parts."

"Exactly. That's the point." She walks her toes up to my cheek. "I want to see you practically naked on a public beach."

"What will you be wearing in this fantasy of yours?"

"You tell me. I bet you've fantasized about seeing me in all sorts of skimpy outfits and probably even more often when I'm naked."

My fantasies are none of her concern. If I told her about them, she might want me to actually do those things. I've known this woman for two days, yet I've already fucked her twice—once four months ago and again today. I will never survive three weeks with her if she traipses about in a skimpy outfit.

"Since you've stopped talking," she says, "I think I'll entertain myself. You can watch out of the corner of your eye if you want."

Though I'm certain I will have a heart attack when I hear the answer, my cock insists that I must find out. "What are you planning to do, Rachelle?"

"Masturbate."

I choke on my own saliva and cough so hard that I'm hacking. "We had sex less than an hour ago. How can you still be randy?"

"Because I'm with you."

"Did you buy a bottle of vodka at the petrol station and drink it all while you were in the loo? Only a drunk woman would do what you just suggested."

She hikes up her skirt and spreads her legs. "What's the verdict? Do you want to watch or not?"

I open my mouth to respond, but then a sign up ahead catches my attention. A sigh of relief rushes out of me. "We're about to cross into London, and it will be only twenty minutes or so until we reach Croydon. We have no time for…messing about."

She tugs her skirt down and rearranges her body so she's properly sitting in her seat.

The closer we get to Croydon, the more excited she is. I don't understand why. We've both visited Poppy Goodburn's bookshop before. By the time we pull into the parking lot behind the shop, the sun is already setting. I hadn't realized how long a day this had been until right now.

As we climb out of the car, I yawn. "We're here, but I don't know if the shop is still open. I hadn't realized how late is."

Rachelle slants forward and squints at the dashboard. Then she sags against her seat. "It's after six. I remember the sign on the door said the bookshop closes at five. We're too late."

"We can come back tomorrow."

"Yeah, I know." She yawns loudly. "Kinda tired, anyway. Probably best if we go to Hugh's flat."

I yawn too. "Yes, I think that is best."

We reach the building where Hugh has his flat and trudge up to the third floor. By the time we reach the door, Rachelle is yawning frequently and clearly too knackered to do anything but sleep. I dig the key out of my pocket and unlock the door, swinging it open.

Rachelle leans against my side, shutting her eyes.

I pick her up and cradle her in my arms as I cross the threshold, then kick the door shut behind me. Since I have never been in Hugh's flat before, I'm not sure where the bedrooms are. I keep Rachelle in my arms as I explore what seems to be the only hallway, discovering two bedrooms there, just as I'd been told there would be. The smaller one would be the guest room, and the larger suite with an enormous bathroom clearly belongs to Lord Sommerleigh. Well, he isn't here right now. I'm certain Hugh wouldn't care if one of us sleeps in his suite.

No, I won't share a bed with Rachelle tonight. She's too sleepy to consent to that. Instead, I go into the larger suite and pull back the covers, then lay her down on the bed. I remove her shoes, but that's all that seems appropriate.

Then I brush hairs away from her face, kiss her forehead, and leave.

Chapter Nine

Rachelle

I wake up in the morning to the aroma of bacon and the sound of someone whistling elsewhere in the flat. I sort of remember Kendall carrying me into the building and into the flat, but after that, things get pretty hazy. I wasn't drunk or on drugs. But I might have gone a little bit crazy in the car with Kendall. Who could blame me? That man is not only smokin' hot but also surprisingly playful. He makes me laugh too.

Still, he must think I'm nuts after what happened yesterday.

When I push the covers off, I realize I'm still wearing the same clothes as yesterday. Yeah, I must have passed out once we got into the flat. I need a shower like I've never needed one before, to wash away all the travel grime. Maybe we only drove two and half hours away, but I still feel grimy—especially after changing my blouse at the petrol station.

The door to my room is open, so maybe I should close it before I undress. But Kendall has seen me naked twice. I don't see how he could possibly be shy about it if he walks into the room while I'm in the buff. So, I strip. Only then do I notice that the bed is enormous. How many people does Hugh Parrish sleep with? The bed seems way too big for just him and Avery. But no, I don't really believe they have orgies in their flat.

I take a moment to turn in a circle and absorb the grandeur of this bedroom. The floor-to-ceiling windows have gauzy drapes that provide just enough privacy without completely blocking the sunshine. I sneak over there to peek through a gap in the curtains. Wow, Hugh and Avery have an incredible view of the city.

Once I've finished gawking, I amble into the bathroom.

Holy shit. It's like a smaller version of a Roman temple, not that I've ever seen one of those in person. I've never seen marble sinks before, but I'm pretty sure the ones in this bathroom are made of that kind of stone, and it looks like the toilet and the open shower stall are as well. Am I really going to take a shower in a stall that has no door or even a curtain? Well, why not?

I glance at the lush wood cabinets and towel racks as I traipse into the shower. Then I need a minute to figure out how to turn on the showerheads. Yeah, there are several of those, each one pointed in a slightly different direction. I manage to adjust the water temperature too, but only after fiddling with various knobs. Finally, the deliciously hot water pours down on me as I pick up a bottle of soap.

Damn, even the sponges are luxurious. Are these real, natural sponges? I think they might be.

"Breakfast will be served in five minutes."

Kendall's voice, coming from inside the bathroom, makes me jump and yelp. The sponge tumbles from my hand as I whirl around. My heart is pounding. Fright will do that to a person. But as I sweep my gaze over Kendall, my heart begins to pound for a different reason. That man looks too damn good in the morning. He ditched his three-piece suit for a pair of khaki pants and a casual blue shirt with the top two buttons undone. His hair is kind of messy too, though in a chic way, not like he forgot to comb his hair.

Wanna jump in the shower with me? That's what my lustful mind wants me to say, but I can't speak. Not when he looks like that.

Kendall takes a slow appraisal of my body, then meets my gaze. "Are you hungry, Rachelle?"

His tone made it clear he's hungry.

Kendall saunters up to me, snatching a towel off the rack along the way, and hands it to me. "Dry off, love. I've made breakfast for you."

"Huh?" I blink swiftly several times but only manage to clear my head enough to speak three words. "I am starved."

"Get dressed, please, and meet me in the kitchen."

He spins around on his heels and marches out of the suite.

I follow his command, which sounds way better in a British accent than it would if an American man had spoken those words. I love American men, but there's just something about Kendall's accent that makes me so horny. Hearing Hugh and Dominic speak doesn't do that to me, though I do love the way Brits talk.

Kendall is the only man I've ever met who would issue an order and make it sound both polite and commanding at the same time. And when I leave the room where I'd slept, I notice another door across the hall that stands partially open. My curiosity gets the better of my manners, and I peek inside that space. It's another, smaller bedroom. Did Kendall sleep in there? I didn't see any evidence that he stayed in the big suite with me.

That man is so unbelievably chivalrous.

As I walk into the main area of the flat, I get my first look at the space. Yeah, I'd been asleep when I arrived here last night. The flat has an open design that I just love, with floor-to-ceiling windows and gauzy drapes, just like the ones in the bedroom suite. The decor has a modern feel and features luscious cream shades, except for the dark-wood shelving that lines one wall. Even the sofa is a cream color.

But when I turn toward the open kitchen, my jaw drops.

Why? Not because of the decor. I can't even focus on that because Kendall stands there, facing away from me, humming while he puts the finishing touches on our breakfast. The precision and fluidity of his movements captures all my attention, and I can't move any closer to the marble bar that stands between us. I just watch him, entranced by his every motion.

He catches me watching him and smiles. "Well, love, are you hungry? I asked you earlier, but you never answered."

"I'm ravenous."

My tummy just grumbled, conveniently backing up my statement and making it seem like I'm starving for food and not him. I want both.

He sets two covered plates on the bar, where two teacups already wait for us alongside a teapot. "Hop on a stool. It's time to eat. And after our adventures yesterday, we both need a hearty breakfast."

I jump onto a stool, only now realizing the kitchen has marble countertops just like the bar. I wriggle my butt, getting comfier than I expected. Stools usually aren't the nicest pieces of furniture to rest your butt on, but this one feels pretty good. "I assume you're talking about our sexual adventures."

"No, I'm referring to everything that happened lately."

Whatever he cooked up smells soooo good. I rub my palms together and inhale the delicious aromas. Then I notice Kendall's expression. He has his brows hiked up and scrunched together over his nose. "Oh, sorry. I'm acting like a weirdo again, aren't I? My behavior yesterday didn't give you much reason to believe I have a brain and know how to use it, or that I'm a mature woman."

"You haven't behaved inappropriately. We both wanted to shag in the car."

"I know. But I got a little wacky afterward, laying sideways in the front seat and asking if you wanted to watch me masturbate."

He comes around to my side of the bar and settles onto the stool next to mine. "Don't worry, Rachelle. I know you are not a lunatic. But I did wonder if you inhaled marijuana fumes while you were in that petrol station. It didn't look like a high-class establishment."

"You're right about that. But I was clean and sober when I acted that way. The only thing that made me high was you."

He smiles in the sweetest shy way. "It has been a bit of a whirlwind since you arrived the other day. I imagine we've both been slightly off kilter since then."

"We're over that hump, aren't we?" I realize what I just said and wince. "That didn't come out the way I meant it."

"I understood your meaning." He clasps my hand, lifting it to his lips to kiss my knuckles. "Today, we will both be calmer and ready for…whatever it is we're doing."

"Yes, we will be calmer. But we'll still have fun." I make a sarcastic show of eying the covered plates. "What's in there? Looks like you're hiding something."

"Nothing dangerous." He plucks the lids off the plates and sets them down. "Have you ever had a fry up?"

"What does that mean in British?"

"The full English breakfast, also known as the fry up or simply the full English. I thought you might enjoy the chance to experience our traditional morning foods."

"I've never had that, so yes, I would love to try it. Can't wait."

"Don't get too excited. It isn't gourmet fare." He points at the plates. "I've used only locally sourced ingredients, to ensure you would have the traditional experience."

It's my turn to lift my brows. "Did you go grocery shopping while I was asleep? Must have slept longer than I realized."

"No, pet, you haven't. I woke early this morning and rang a chap I know who owns a shop that specializes in local items. He had someone deliver the groceries about an hour ago."

"You cooked all this in an hour?" When he nods, I can't help gaping at him. "I thought you were the butler at Sommerleigh House, not the cook."

"I don't create the meals that the Parrishes eat, but I have cultivated relationships with grocers and bakers and butchers, as well as pâtisseries." I must seem confused because he explains, "A pâtisserie is a shop that sells French pastries."

"The Parrishes don't seem like the snobby type."

Kendall rests a hand on my knee. "They are not snobby. But when I suggested Sommerleigh should support local shops and artisans, they agreed it would be a smashing idea. When Hugh moved into this flat, I cultivated relationships with London shops as well."

"You do a lot more than open and close doors for people, don't you? I had no idea. It's no wonder the Parrishes love you."

"They have been extraordinarily good to me. I'm simply returning the favor." He pushes a plate toward me. "Now, it's time for your introduction to the full English."

I study the food on my plate, and my mouth starts to water. I'm even hungrier than I realized.

Kendall points at each dish in turn. "You have back bacon, poached eggs, Cumberland sausage, baked beans, fried tomatoes, fried mushrooms, and black pudding, along with both fried bread and the toasted sort with marmalade. I would normally include bubble and squeak, but that wasn't possible today."

"Uh, what is bubble and squeak? And why wasn't it possible?"

"Bubble and squeak is leftovers, essentially. I don't have that since this is our first meal here in this flat."

"Right. That makes sense."

He pours a measure of milk into our cups before adding the tea. Like a true gentleman, he asks if I want sugar and how much of it I want.

"Just two spoonfuls, Kendall, thank you."

"My pleasure." He slides his plate closer to himself. "Go on, Rachelle, try the food. If you despise it, I won't be offended. The full English isn't something most Americans appreciate."

I cut off a chunk of sausage and put it in my mouth. "Mm, this is better than I expected." Next, I try each of the other dishes one by one and voice my approval, which makes Kendall sit up straighter and smile with satisfaction. "This is all so delicious. You're an incredible cook."

"But you haven't tried the black pudding." He puckers his lips and folds his arms over his chest. "You think it's disgusting, don't you?"

"I didn't say a word."

"True, but your entire face twisted into an expression of sheer revulsion."

Yeah, okay, he's got me on that one. "I'm being so rude. You made all this food for me, and I should at least try the black pudding."

One side of his mouth kinks upward. "I was having you on. Eat the pudding or don't, I will not be offended either way."

"I see. Well, I'd still like to try it." I take a bite of the black pudding and chew it slowly. "Tastes kind of meaty and nutty, but it has the texture of salami. Not bad, but I won't be begging you to cook it for me again. Do you like this stuff?"

He shrugs. "I grew up eating it."

"That's not an affirmative answer."

"I don't particularly enjoy it. But I wanted you to have the traditional full English experience."

"And I appreciate that." I lean over to kiss his cheek. "Thank you, Kendall."

He bows his head to focus on his food, shoving both fried tomatoes and fried mushrooms into his mouth at the same time.

I munch on some fried bread, somewhat surprised by how good it tastes. Then I gobble up bacon and baked beans, all while Kendall keeps shoving food into his mouth in what seem like odd combinations. Beans and marmalade toast. Sausage and marmalade, without the toast. Finally, he thrusts a mouthful of beans, poached eggs, and black pudding into his mouth. *Yech.*

He catches me looking at him and glances sideways at me. With a full mouth, he says, "What? Do I have marmalade on my chin?"

"No." I tip my head to the side, studying him. "Do you always eat like this? You seem like the tidy type, but you're currently sucking up food like an industrial vacuum cleaner."

He finishes off his mouthful of food and carefully dabs his lips clean. "I am unusually hungry this morning, that's all."

"Mm-hm. Now tell me the real reason you're eating that way."

Kendall picks up his teacup and gulps down the remaining liquid inside it. Then he swipes the back of his hand across his mouth. "I suppose I'm reverting to my old self, the bloke I used to be before the elder Lord Sommerleigh hired me to work for him."

"Why are you doing that?"

He rests his elbow on the bar and sets his forehead in his raised hand. Kendall mumbles something I can't understand.

I slide an arm around his shoulders. With my head near his, I murmur, "No idea what you just said. You're mumbling into your hand."

He lowers his arm but still won't look at me. "I'm behaving like… Well, not myself. Or at least, not the me I've become over the past seventeen years."

"Which version is the real you?"

"Both."

"You aren't going to tell me about the old you yet."

He straightens and slings an arm around my waist to pull me closer. "Not just yet. Is that all right?"

"Yep. I can wait."

Chapter Ten

Kendall

After we finish our breakfast, we head for Poppy's bookshop. I insist upon driving. When Rachelle asks why, I inform her, "You are a guest in my country, which means it's my duty to ensure you have a good experience here. And also, you would probably drive on the wrong side of the road." Though she repeatedly assures me that she would not do that, I still insist upon doing all the driving.

"Fine by me," she declares. "Why should I care? I'll get a better view of London as a passenger."

"Indeed you will. And I promise to point out anything of interest."

Rachelle settles onto her seat and gazes out the window as if everything she sees is the most fascinating thing in the world. I point out the butcher's shop that provided the meat for our breakfast and the bakery that provided the bread. None of that information seems thrilling to me, but she becomes rather excited when she sees those establishments.

We arrive at Poppy's bookshop early enough that the place isn't chockablock with customers. I can't help wincing faintly as I push through the door, holding it open for Rachelle. If she notices that, she at least has the good manners not to comment on it. I don't know why I'm anxious. Well, all right, I do know. The first time I was in this shop, I had been overrun by people demanding all sorts of things that I couldn't find or about which I knew nothing.

Today will be different.

Rachelle gives me a quick kiss. "Relax. You're a visitor today, not the man in charge." She clasps my hand firmly as we approach the sales counter, where Owen and Poppy stand on the other side. "Good morning. It's a gorgeous day, isn't it?"

"Yes, it is a lovely morning," Poppy agrees. "We're so glad you two stopped by to see us. Hugh and Avery mentioned that you would be taking three weeks off to enjoy London and get to know each other better."

The phrase "enjoy London" suddenly has another meaning altogether—for me, at least. I can't stop reliving in my mind what we did in the car yesterday.

Rachelle nudges me with her elbow. "Wake up, Kendall. Owen asked you a question."

"What? Oh. Sorry." I wince again. "What was the question?"

Owen chuckles. "The uptight butler has it bad for a girl, so much that he can't think straight. About damn time."

Why is it a good thing that I'm scatterbrained? Owen is barmy. Or maybe I am. Though I want my relationship with Rachelle to work, the odds are that I will cock it up.

I abruptly realize the conversation has moved on.

Rachelle has been talking to Owen. "Yes, absolutely. I would love to read one of your steamy romance novels. Can you recommend one for me to start with?"

"Sure thing. But why don't you come around to this side of the counter and chat with Poppy while Kendall and I pick the right book for you."

"That's a great idea."

She can't honestly think my opinion of romance novels will be helpful to her. I've given her no reason to believe that. It's more likely that she wants to chat with another woman, rather than just me.

Owen slaps my back—twice. "Come on, Kendall. Let's find a book for Rachelle."

He winks.

I have no bloody idea what that means.

Owen leads me over to a display at the front of the shop, where books are displayed on a large table in small piles or propped up on little stands. Every book bears the name Desiree Lachance. These are Owen's romance novels.

He waves an arm toward the display. "These are my most recent books." He waves his arm toward the wall. "If you look over there, you'll see my backlist titles. I have a lot of them."

"I can see that. You're quite prolific."

"So, you probably have no idea what sort of stories Rachelle might like the best."

"Afraid so. But she does like, ah…" No, I can't tell him that. It's embarrassing.

Owen grins. "I bet I can guess what she likes. Your hesitation tells me everything I need to know." He walks round to the other side of the table and plucks up a book. "Here you go. *The Duchess and the Butler*. This is my first steamy historical. Well, my first historical, period."

I reach across the table to take the hardcover. "You just happen to have written a book about a butler?" If I sound skeptical, that's because I bloody well am. When I flip the book open to check the copyright page, I narrow my gaze on Owen. "You published the story this year. When, precisely?"

"I wrote it three months ago and published the story four weeks ago."

No, he couldn't have… It's preposterous, but his smirk makes me suspicious. "Did you write this about me?"

"Sort of. I used you as my template for an efficient, upstanding butler. That's how I know Rachelle will love this book."

"And what precisely are the duchess and the butler doing in this story?"

Owen chuckles again. "What do you think? Let's just say they aren't folding the laundry."

"You mean they're shagging."

He points a finger at me. "You got it. This book has the most steamy scenes of any of my novels."

"I can't give this book to Rachelle."

"Of course you can." He moves closer to me, setting a hand on my shoulder, and speaks in a hushed voice. "Everybody knows that you two humped like wild bunnies when you first met. If you wanted it to be a secret, you shouldn't have screwed in the Mercedes with Arthur in the front seat."

"Your point being…"

"Rachelle will love this book." He snatches it from my hand so he can slap the tome on my chest. "Read the steamy parts to her. Read them aloud, Kendall. Take the word of the romance writer. I'm an expert on writing erotic scenes."

He might have a point. But no, I can't do what he suggested.

Owen winks at me again. "Tell you what. Take this book and try out my suggestion. If it doesn't work, the book is yours at no charge. If it does work, then you'll owe me sixteen ninety-nine—in British pounds, naturally."

"I will pay for it upfront to support Poppy's bookshop."

"See? I knew you were an upstanding guy. But I doubt Poppy will allow you to pay for the book."

"I'll try anyway."

When I glance at the sales counter, I realize I cannot walk over there while holding this item. It wouldn't be a surprise if Rachelle sees it. But what if she doesn't like the book Owen chose? *Buck up, you moron. You know you want to read a steamy romance to Rachelle.* Yes, I do. Desperately. But if she doesn't like the way I read it, or if she thinks I'm ridiculous, I might just crawl into the boot of the Jaguar and stay there for the duration of our holiday.

No, I will not. I'm a forty-three-year-old man, for pity's sake. No longer will I allow my past to seep into my present and make me freeze up.

But I do still have the problem of how to surprise Rachelle when I'm holding the book in plain view. So, I turn to Owen. "Could you give me a paper sack so I can hide this book inside it?"

"Sure thing." He starts to walk toward the bookshelves on the wall, beckoning me to follow. "This is the best route to bypass the ladies. Better tuck that book under your shirt just to be safe."

Since I've worn my shirt untucked today, I easily slide the book inside it, cradling the tome to my belly. Then I follow Owen round the far side of the shop. Poppy and Rachelle are engaged in a lively conversation with a pair of elderly women, which seems to center on recommendations for steamy romance novels.

Owen smiles and rolls his eyes. "Those two ladies are my biggest fans, though they don't know it yet. I'm still mulling over the idea of outing myself publicly. My friends and family know I'm Desiree Lachance, but nobody else does."

"Are you worried your fans might desert you if they find out a man writes those novels?"

"Of course I am. But that anxiety lessens more every day, thanks to Poppy. She supports me in whatever decision I make about revealing my pen name."

For reasons I can't explain, I tell him something I shouldn't. "Yes, I can relate to your dilemma. My previous career was far more humiliating than your erotic romances."

"In what way?"

"Well, it's...nothing. Forget I mentioned it."

We've just reached the far end of the sales counter, so Owen scurries off to find a plain paper sack that will fit this hardcover novel.

Rachelle glances at me and smiles.

I try to return the expression, but my smile comes out rather tight.

She blows me a kiss.

And I bow my head, though my lips curl up a touch and I can't stop myself from glancing at her sideways. I am behaving like a ruddy schoolboy.

Owen returns with a paper sack in his hand. He opens it up and holds out the sack so I can slide the book inside it. Then he folds the top over and offers me the package. "Your secret is safe until you're ready to reveal it to Rachelle."

"Thank you, Owen."

He rises onto the tips of his toes to survey the shop and especially the area where Poppy stands behind the counter. "Looks like business is picking up. I should get over there and pitch in."

"Of course. Thank you again for suggesting this book."

"No problem."

He jogs over to Poppy, and Rachelle approaches me.

"Are you ready to go?" I ask. "It seems that the shop is getting busier."

"Since we don't want to get in the way, I told Poppy we'll be heading out now to do some sightseeing."

We make our way out of the shop and to the car park where we left the Jaguar. As we're settling in, with me in the driver's seat, I ask Rachelle, "Where would you like to go next?"

"I know it's not a thrilling option, but I've always loved art galleries."

"How about the National Gallery? It's quite large, and it's right on Trafalgar Square."

"Sounds fantastic. Let's go there."

Our trip to the National Gallery seems to enthrall Rachelle, considering the way she races about in Trafalgar Square to see every last corner of it. She dips her hands into the fountain nearest to the museum, the one that spurts water high above our heads, and she loves the mermaids that spit water from their mouths. She peppers me with questions, but I can't answer any of them. I'm hardly an expert on water fountains or the construction of Trafalgar Square and the buildings around it. I've never been enchanted by artwork either, yet I find myself getting immersed in the historic paintings and sculptures just as much as Rachelle does.

Since the moment I met her, I've had trouble believing she is thirty-nine years old. Of course, most people assume I'm in my twenties, though I passed that mark a long time ago. Only Rosalyn, the Dowager Lady Sommerleigh, knows my true age—and now so does Rachelle. I'm not embarrassed by my age, but it never seemed important to share that information.

Rachelle spends ten minutes studying a painting created by an artist called Jean-Auguste-Dominique Ingres. When I ask why that artwork captivates her, she slides her arm round my waist and gazes up at me with a soft, sweet expression. "It's simple. I love this painting because of the dress."

"The dress? I don't understand."

She points at the woman in the painting. "Her flower-print dress. It's gorgeous."

"Oh. That's not the sort of thing I would pay any mind to."

"No kidding. Most men wouldn't be interested unless her breasts were hanging out."

When we stop to admire a painting by Peter Paul Rubens, whose name I do recognize unlike that other artist, I find this artwork far more intriguing than the one Rachelle had loved because of the flower-print dress. The image depicts Samson and Delilah. I assume that the man who lies draped over Delilah's legs must be Samson, at any rate. It's a dramatic and complex painting, and I'm surprised by the elements in the background that add another layer to the artwork.

"You really like this painting, huh?" Rachelle says. "You've been staring at it for one minute longer than I stared at the woman in the flower dress."

"Have I? Yes, this painting does intrigue me."

She clucks her tongue. "I'm so disappointed to find out you're a typical man."

"In what way?"

"You like this painting because Delilah's breast is on full display."

"No, that's not the reason I like it."

She taps a finger on my nose. "Admit it. You like seeing a woman's tit."

"Only because the artistry is impressive."

Rachelle clamps her teeth down on her lips, trying to squelch her laughter, but it emerges anyway—as unladylike snorts. Not that I give a toss if she behaves in a ladylike manner.

She pats my cheek while giving me a teasing smile. "Oh, yeah, the *artistry* is excellent."

"Yes, it is. At least I wasn't enthralled by a flower-print dress."

"Maybe later I'll lie on a chaise with my tit hanging out, just to get your attention."

"No need for that. Your body always has my full attention." I check the time on my mobile. "It's nearly one o'clock. Shall we eat now or later?"

"Now. I'm famished."

We enjoy a lovely lunch at a French bistro, though I feel compelled to point out to her how odd it is that she came to England so she could eat French food. She knows I'm teasing her. I love doing that. She always laughs and smiles when I say something cheeky.

After lunch, I inquire about where she would like to go next.

"Don't know. You're my tour guide, Kendall, so give me some options, please."

"Ah… I've essentially used up all my ideas. Sightseeing has never been a part of my life until now."

"How can a man live in London all his life but know so little about it?"

I slap her arse. "Careful, or I might drag you into the backseat of the Jaguar again."

"Oh, darn, that would be awful."

But no, I won't do that now. I'm enjoying our sightseeing too much. "There is something I've heard of that's rather outlandish."

"That sounds intriguing. What is this outlandish thing?"

"The London Dungeon. It's a tour of the most hideous and frightening times in the city's past."

"Ooh, that does sound intriguing." She snuggles up to me. "Will you hold me if I get too scared?"

"Can't picture you ever getting that scared. But yes, I will comfort you—anytime, anywhere."

We drive to a car park near the attraction since the London Dungeon has no car park of its own. Then we walk to the entrance hand in hand. I can't believe I am visiting an outrageous attraction like this one, a place designed to frighten and thrill people who are easily frightened and thrilled. I might be slightly skeptical of how much fun this will be, but I'm certain I will not scream or faint. Neither will Rachelle. She's a brave woman.

And I love that about her.

The most enjoyable part of our excursion is seeing the way she reacts to the various elements of this tour. Water rides aren't usually something I like, but the boat ride that begins our journey is rather fun. I never would have believed something called The Torture Chamber could be entertaining, but surprisingly, it is. We go through fifteen segments of the tour before we reach the last thrill ride, one that requires a bar to hold us in our seats for a death-defying plunge.

Rachelle shrieks with joy.

And, well, I...laugh and whoop. Can't believe I did that.

This woman makes me want to do any barmy thing as long as she's with me.

Chapter Eleven

Rachelle

Wow, the London Dungeon was a hoot. I'm amazed that Kendall enjoyed it as much as I did, since he claimed the excursion wouldn't thrill him at all. He told me that because he didn't want me to be disappointed if he seemed unimpressed. But he loved our gory, raucous adventure. And he even whooped during the big drop.

I really need to take him to Six Flags in Missouri.

"What is Six Flags?" he asks when I mention my idea. "I assume it's some sort of amusement park, but I've never heard of it."

"You were right. It is an amusement park. There's a chain of them scattered around the mainland United States, including one about two hours away from my hometown."

"Perhaps one day, you'll take me there. To your hometown and to Six Flags."

A feeling of euphoria rushes through me briefly. Why should I feel that way simply because Kendall suggested he might want to go home with me? He didn't vow to marry me.

The last stop on the London Dungeon tour is the tavern. I have a delicious cocktail called Hex on the Beach while Kendall tries something called Ripper's Revenge. I almost chose the Plague Tonic but changed my mind when I saw Hex on the Beach on the menu. Kendall invites me to taste his drink, but I decline. I'm enjoying my cocktail too much.

As we leave the London Dungeon, Kendall swings our joined hands and whistles a cheerful tune. He smiles too, with a genuine sweetness that melts my heart. I need to spend more time with him, and we have three weeks to do that. We agree that we're both too tired for more sightseeing today, so Kendall drives us back to Hugh's flat. This time, he doesn't need to carry my unconscious body across the threshold. I'm fully awake.

Despite the fact that I'm conscious, Kendall insists on picking me up and carrying me over to the sofa, where he drops me onto the cushions from behind. He then shuts the front door and leaps over the sofa, whumping down beside me.

He lays his arm across the sofa's back, inviting me to snuggle up.

I can't resist that invitation. Once I have myself tucked against him, I rest my cheek on his chest. "You know what? I'm not even sure what day it is. My London holiday has been a whirlwind so far."

"You want to know what day it is? I haven't a clue." Kendall whips out his cell phone and fiddles with stuff on the screen. He freezes. His eyes widen. "Bollocks."

"What's wrong?"

"I checked the calender on my mobile. Three weeks from yesterday will be Halloween."

"Yeah. Why does that shock you?"

He bows his head, covering his face with one hand, and sighs heavily. "I forgot to give Lord and Lady Sommerleigh the itinerary for the Halloween soiree."

"Itinerary? It's a party, right? I thought those kind of events were low-key and didn't require event planning."

He throws his head back, letting it fall onto the sofa. "But I always meticulously plan and manage the Halloween soiree. They won't even know where to find my itinerary."

"Relax, Kendall. I'm sure they can manage. But if you're really worried, just call Hugh and tell him about the itinerary."

"I don't want to bother them."

"Just make the call. Do it now."

He sighs and excavates his cell phone from his pants pocket, then dials the number. I can hear it ringing faintly. He sits up straighter. "Arthur? Why are you answering the phone? Oh, I see. Yes, of course that makes sense." He glances at me, and I give him the thumbs-up sign. Kendall clears his throat. "May I speak to Lord or Lady Sommerleigh, please? It's important." Kendall holds the phone to his chest. "Arthur is fetching one of them for me."

"Great. You'll feel a lot better once you know your itinerary is in the right hands."

A tinny voice emerges from his phone, slightly muffled by his chest. He jerks the phone up to his ear. "Arthur? Oh, it's you, Lady Sommerleigh. Yes, I did need to speak with you. What? It's about the itinerary for the Halloween soiree. I forgot to tell you about that before Rachelle and I left on our holiday."

He seems more relaxed already. Just knowing his precious plans for the party are not in danger of falling apart has made him feel better. I knew it would. Can't expect a super-professional butler and party planner not to get a teeny bit anxious about his well-laid plans.

Suddenly, Kendall snaps upright. "What? That isn't on my itinerary." His eyes have gone wild, and his lips have fallen open. "But the plan—Yes, of course, it is your party." Kendall slumps against the sofa again. "Well, I'm glad to hear that. But I wish someone had warned me about the change, that's all. I had everything planned out with bulleted lists and—All right. Thank you, Lady Sommerleigh. Ah, yes. Thank you, *Avery*."

Kendall ends the call and wipes a hand over his face.

"How bad was it?" I ask. "Did they turn your carefully laid plans into an outrageous spectacle?"

"Not quite. But my tasteful soiree has become a 'Halloween bash for the ages,' according to Avery. Not sure which ages Lady Sommerleigh was referring to."

"Well, I'd guess it won't be a plague party."

He eyes me sideways and smirks. "No, we did that already. The London Dungeon was quite an experience."

"Yep. But now, I just want to eat something, take a shower, and go to bed." I lean over to rest my chin on his shoulder. "I'd like to do all of those things with you."

"I would love to eat, shower, and sleep with you. Not all at the same time, though."

My mind conjures a vision of the two of us in the shower, eating croissants, and then we slide down onto the shower floor to sleep. Now that's a dumb fantasy. Don't know why my stupid brain thought I wanted to picture soggy croissants.

A steamy shower with Kendall would be nice, though.

Kendall kisses the top of my head. "I would love to shower with you, pet. But first, I need to feed you."

"Maybe we should order a pizza. You must be as tired as I am."

He yawns. "Yes, all right. Let's do that."

We spend five minutes discussing what we like on pizza, and it turns out we have similar tastes. Neither of us likes anything spicy, but we both love extra cheese for that super-gooey yum factor. Kendall would never describe it that way, but he grins when I say the words. Once our pizza arrives, we have fun feeding each other. But we have even more fun in the shower. I bet no one else realizes how playful and funny the supposedly uptight butler can be. We don't have sex, but that's fine by me.

Just being with him is enough.

We bathed together in the gigantic shower in the main suite. But when it's time to go to bed, Kendall dries us both off with big, plush towels and then starts to walk out of the suite.

"Where are you going, Kendall?"

He pauses on the threshold of the suite's doorway, turning only his head to look at me. "I'm going to my room. Have a good night's sleep, Rachelle."

"Uh-uh, no way. You are not scurrying away to that smaller room to sleep alone. We've had sex multiple times, and that means you can and should share this ginormous bed with me." When his face pinches up a teeny bit, I sit down on the bed's edge and pat the mattress. "Come over here, Kendall. A big, sexy man like you needs a large bed. And besides, I want to spoon with you. Kind of hard to do that when you're in another room."

He stares at me for about three seconds, then he gives in and saunters over to the bed. "Which side do you prefer?"

"Don't care."

He picks me up and tosses me into the middle of the bed. Then the world's hottest butler crawls across the mattress to lie down beside me. He pats my bottom. "Roll over, love. Can't spoon with you when you're on your back."

"You're the one who tossed me here." I flip onto my side. "Ready now. Let the spooning begin."

Kendall stretches out on his side behind me and wriggles closer until his body is molded to mine. A long sigh rushes out of him. "Never realized how wonderful this would feel."

"You've never spooned before?"

"No."

"I had one boyfriend who liked spooning, but he dumped me for his best friend. I should've guessed they were more than just best buddies who loved to go to football games together. I mean, they would feed each other loaded nachos. That should've been a clue, but I overlooked it." It's my turn to sigh, but it's not a relaxed sound. "Getting dumped for another guy isn't great for a girl's ego."

"I'm sorry that happened to you. Getting thrown over is never a pleasant experience."

"How many times has it happened to you?"

"Too many. But I'd rather not discuss my failed relationships tonight."

"Sure. I understand."

The feel of Kendall's body cradled against me chases away all the bad memories. The warmth of him, the scent of him, I love everything about this man. We had so much fun today, more fun than I've ever had with anyone else.

I don't know exactly when I fell asleep, but the next thing I know, I'm waking up to golden sunshine filtering into the room through the gauzy curtains and the feel of Kendall's body still molded to mine. Don't want to move even one inch. I'd rather lie here with my eyes closed and revel in the simple pleasure of being in bed with a man who appreciates me. I appreciate him too. Big time.

Kendall nuzzles my ear. "Are you awake, pet?"

"Mm-hm. Are you awake?"

"Cheeky girl." He kisses a path up my throat, making me shiver in the best way. "I'll make breakfast while you figure out what sights you want to see today."

"Not worried about the Halloween bash anymore, hey?"

"Sod the Halloween bash." He nibbles on my earlobe. "Lord and Lady Sommerleigh have an excellent staff and many mates who will help them."

I roll onto my back so I can gaze into his beautiful blue eyes. "Are you also not worried about what the American Wives Club might do?"

He lets his head fall down, his chin nudging his chest, and blows out a long sigh. "Bollocks. I forgot about that."

"I suggest you keep on forgetting. Strategic amnesia can be useful."

"Perhaps you're right." He sits up and stretches, yawning in a way that seems like a joke to me. When he closes one hand around my breast, I know for sure he's joking, especially when he cups the bottom of my breast and jiggles it. "I do love your tits."

"I love your dick, so we're even."

"What would you like to do today and for the rest of our long holiday?"

"That's a big open question. For today, I think I'd like to see stereotypical touristy stuff. You know, like Big Ben and the Tower Bridge."

Kendall shakes his head, pretending to be disappointed. "I can show you much better stereotypical British monuments."

"Great. I'll go anywhere with you, my sexy tour guide."

"And I will take you anywhere, my sexy tourist."

Kendall and I whip up a hearty breakfast together, then we head out to the places he suggests will give me the best idea of what London, and England in general, is like. We hop in the London Eye, a giant wheel that has pods attached to it so tourists like me can get the best view of the city. Kendall also recommends Madame Toussaud's, and though I don't expect to enjoy a wax museum, I wind up having a "cracking" time, as my tour guide says. Wax versions of famous people are weird and sort of creepy, but it's the ultimate kitschy experience.

As we're ambling down a street, holding hands, I ask him, "Were you born in London?"

"Yes."

"Do your parents still live here?"

He tenses up just a little, but it's enough to prove to me he doesn't like discussing his family. "Yes, Mum and Dad live in London, though not in a posh neighborhood like the one we're currently enjoying."

"Where do they live?" When his expression tightens even more, I relent. "Sorry. It's none of my business."

"Perhaps I'll tell you about them another time. This is meant to be a fun holiday for you."

"Okay. I can wait."

For the next week, Kendall shows me his world—London and the neighboring areas. We visit parks and museums, shops and attractions, anything that my tour guide thinks will be a cracking experience for me. Yeah, I've adopted that British word. It's fun to say. I also like the word blimey, but I decide not to start spouting that one, at least not yet. I don't want Kendall to think I'm mocking him.

One day, while we're ambling through a beautiful park, I tell him something that makes him blush. No, it's nothing dirty. "I love your voice, Kendall. Not only is it deep and sexy, but your British accent is the hottest thing ever."

"Hottest ever? That's rubbish. I'm sure you can think of many other things that are sexier than my voice and accent."

"Nope, I can't. Scoured the internet for any other man who's hotter than you, and Google told me you're officially the hottest British man on the planet. You're tied with Chris Hemsworth for hottest man overall."

"Only tied?" He makes a sarcastic sniffing sound. "I'm afraid I'll have to put you on the next flight back to America. I can't be with a woman who thinks an actor is hotter than I am."

I grin and bump my shoulder into his bicep. "You just admitted you *are* hot."

He twists his mouth into an expression that seems like he's desperately trying not to grin. And he changes the subject. "Shall we have lunch at the flat? Or would you prefer to eat out?"

"Let's eat in this time."

I love cooking with him, showering with him, laughing with him, sightseeing with him, and so much more. But before I know it, two weeks have flown by.

This morning, we both agreed that we'd like to take a few days off from sightseeing and just hang out together in the flat like true couch potatoes. Kendall makes a joke about me being "a steamy hot potato," but as soon as he speaks those words, he abruptly turns serious.

"I have something I meant to show you," he says. "Owen convinced me to buy it, but I've been reticent to share this item with you."

"We've gotten to know each other pretty well lately. You ought to know by now that you can tell me anything."

"In that case, I'll fetch the item."

He dashes into the bedroom suite and returns a moment later carrying a brown paper bag. He hops over the sofa's back, whumping down right beside me, and offers me the package. His excitement is clear and palpable, and I've never seen him this way before. When he hands me the bag, his smile broadens. "It's a gift for you. If you don't like it, I won't be offended."

I'm still amazed by his chameleon-like ability to be uber-professional and mature one minute, then shy and sweet the next, and now as excited as a kid at Christmas. But he's giving me a gift, and I can't wait to see what it is.

As I accept the bag, he leans forward and taps his fingers on his thigh. "Go on, then. Open it."

"Okay, okay, hold your horses." I open the bag and pull out… "A book?"

Chapter Twelve

Kendall

Rachelle seems less than elated by my gift. Perhaps I had hoped she would be more excited by what I've given her, but then, she hasn't seen what it actually is yet. She knows it's a book, but not what genre or which author. I probably should have led with that. With my planning skills, I know better than to simply shove the book in her face and expect her to leap for joy.

"Yes, it's a book," I confirm. "But you've got it the wrong way round. That's the back cover."

"Right, I see that now." She flips the book over, and her brows shoot up. "A romance novel? Oh, I get it. The author is Desiree Lachance."

"Which is Owen Metzger's pen name. He recommended this book."

The cover features a couple dressed in what looks like eighteenth-century garb, though I'm hardly an expert on antique garments. The clothing is lovely, but it's the bloke with his shirt ripped open who grabs Rachelle's attention. She can't seem to tear her focus away from the cover model's muscles. His companion is a beautiful blonde.

"It's a clinch cover," I inform her, quite proud of myself for learning the term. "That means the woman and the bloke are embracing passionately."

"Yeah, I could've figured that out just from looking at the cover image. That's one hot clinch. I mean, the woman's boobs are almost spilling out of her gown." Rachelle finally reads the words on the cover, and her brows lift again. "*The Duchess and the Butler?* Did Owen write this about you?"

"He wrote this book after meeting me. But he never did explicitly state whether I was the inspiration for this novel. I don't see how I could be."

"Why would you say that?"

I make a face that Rachelle would call "scrunching up" but that I would describe as my bloody stupid way of expressing discomfort with the topic at hand. "Owen barely knows me, and I am not the sort of butler depicted in this book."

"Did you read it?"

"No." I squirm and avoid looking at her because the truth is humiliating. "But I downloaded the audiobook version and listened to several chapters."

"I bet the narrator doesn't have anywhere near as sexy a voice as you do."

"The narrator is a woman."

She feigns disgust. "How could he not have hired you to read that novel? It's a travesty."

"Owen did suggest that I should, ah, read the book to you."

Rachelle grins. "Now that's a fabulous idea. Read me some of it now."

"Perhaps I should cook dinner first. You must famished."

"Nope. Not hungry yet." She wriggles closer. "Read me that novel now, Kendall, please."

I know she won't give up until I do what she asked, and strangely, I realize I want to read this book to her. But... "I can't promise that hearing me speak the words in this book will be a pleasant experience. I've never narrated anything, unless reading a grocery list aloud counts."

"Oh, it absolutely does—for you. Other guys, not so much. If you rattled off the list of components inside a computer, that would make me hot for sure."

"You are a bizarre woman, but I shall give you what you want."

She wriggles about again, nearly elbowing me in the face in the process, while she struggles to get into a cross-legged position facing me. "I'm ready. Lay some steamy goodness on me."

Rachelle might well be disappointed by my effort, but I will give it a go. So, I open the book to the first chapter, clear my throat, and begin. "Letitia, Duchess of Waystorm, lay sprawled on her chaise in the morning room, dreaming of a lover who did not exist. Her husband's passing two months ago had resulted in a flurry of men coming to court the wealthy heiress. But she wanted only one man—the one she had dreamed of every night, her perfect lover."

"Skip ahead to the steamy parts."

"Don't you want to hear the whole story? You won't understand what's going on if you skip ahead."

"Don't care. Find a hot scene and perform it for me."

I stare at her without blinking. "Perform it? I am not an actor."

"Oh, come on, do this for me." She slides a hand down my inner thigh. "Pretend I'm the duchess and you're the butler. I know that's a stretch for you."

"You sly chit. All right, I will try to narrate this in a way that's, ah…steamy. Whatever that means."

She pokes my thigh with one finger. "You know very well what 'steamy' means. The man who screwed me in cars twice can't be shy about sex."

"Yes, you're right. I'll do my best."

"Imagine you're the butler in the book who's trying to seduce the widowed and very horny duchess."

My brows lift. "The text doesn't specify that she's randy."

"How do you know? You've only read three lines."

"That's true." I raise the book again and flip through the pages until I find what Rachelle wants. Then I clear my throat. "Gideon had just finished clearing the table in the solar when the Duchess sauntered into the room and sprawled on a chaise. Her bosom nearly spilled out of her—"

"Hold on, Kendall." Rachelle gusts out a big, sarcastic sigh. "You aren't really trying, are you? Maybe you need visual aids."

"Of what sort?"

She grasps my hand, then molds it to her bosom. "This kind. Now try it again. And please, don't skimp on the steam. Your voice should be dripping with it, like honey sitting on a window sill, getting warm and liquid, then the bottle falls over and the honey drizzles onto—"

"Yes, I understood what you wanted." If she speaks in that sultry voice again, I'll fuck her right here on the sofa in front of the picture windows. The drapes are pulled back, so someone might see us. Oddly, I do want to ravish her that way. Well, I suppose it isn't that odd since I've done something similar twice before. "Let me continue, please, without the commentary."

"Sure. I'm all ears." She makes a zipper motion across her mouth.

"Her bosom nearly spilled out of her bodice, and she licked her lips with a hunger that made Gideon hard in an instant." I frown at the text. "No man gets an erection in an instant. Owen should know that, yet he writes about Gideon going hard instantly. It's rubbish."

"Owen is a great writer."

"But he's using ridiculous hyperbole."

She throws her hands up and growls. "Are you going to get me hot and bothered, or would you rather complain about Gideon's erection? This is a romance novel, not a scientific treatise on male arousal."

"I'm sorry, love. Let me try again." I take a drink from my water glass and make another attempt. "He couldn't resist poring his gaze over her while imagining all the ways he might take her. On the chaise. On the Persian rug. Up against the solar windows. Most decadently of all, he felt a fervent need to drag her into the foyer and fuck her on the floor."

"That was great, Kendall. But add more steam. Don't be shy about it."

"He wanted Letitia so badly that he didn't care about the scandal that inevitably would erupt if anyone discovered their forbidden affair. 'I need you inside me, Gideon, right now,' the duchess declared, her bosom heaving with her desire for him. 'Yes, my love, I need you as well,' he said, 'for only your lust can satiate my carnal appetite.' "

I need to pause for a moment, so that I won't develop an erection myself, just like Gideon in the book. Mine won't happen in an instant. But reading these erotic phrases to Rachelle is getting me randier by the minute.

"Please keep going, Kendall. You're in the groove now."

When I resume narrating, I can't believe how rough and deep my voice has become, and I can tell she loves it. But I skip ahead in the text, strictly so I won't come in my trousers. "Letitia's gown fell to the floor in a pool of lacy fabric, exposing her entire body to Gideon. No words were necessary. They knew what they wanted from each other, and nothing could stop the tidal wave of desire. He lay her down on a chaise longue and spread her thighs for him, revealing the shimmering proof of her hunger for him. Then he lowered his mouth to her folds and—"

I shut the book.

Rachelle jerks. "What are you doing? You can't stop in the middle of a hot scene."

"I'm exercising the time-honored art of the cliffhanger."

"Time-honored? What baloney." She smacks my arm. "You're having fun torturing me, aren't you?"

"Not at all." I keep hold of the book to ensure she can't snatch it away. "If you want to hear the rest of the story, first you'll need to give me what I want."

"And that is…"

I slip an arm round her waist and tug her close until our lips hover a hair's breadth apart. "You must have noticed my erection. Reading those lines about Letitia's hunger made me so fucking randy that I need to shag you."

"Oh. Well, in that case…" She nabs the book and flings it away. The tome smacks down halfway to the kitchen. "My body is yours. Wanna do it on the sofa?"

"No, I have a better idea." I move her onto my lap, then stand up. She knows what I want her to do, so I have no need to tell her to wrap her legs round me. "Let's try that unusual thing again, this time in a posh bedroom suite that offers plenty of room for anything we want to try."

"Hugh did say his flat is our flat."

"Shall we go into the bedroom, then?"

"Yes, absolutely."

I carry her into the bedroom suite and use my foot to push the covers out of the way. Then I lay her down on the silky sheets, which might actually be silk. But no fabric on earth could feel as soft as her skin. The first time we had tried this maneuver, it seemed strange and awkward, though we managed to get each other off quite well once we mastered the position. Today, we won't need to adjust. We both know how this will go.

And it should be much easier on a large mattress.

While I crawl onto the bed, Rachelle writhes like a lustful serpent. "You never told me what this move is called or how you came up with the idea."

"It wasn't my idea. I found it on a website." Lying down beside her, I turn onto my side. "There was a time when I hoped learning more inventive sexual positions might make women want more than a brief acquaintance with me. It didn't work. They still found me uninspiring."

"That's crazy. You are inspiring in every way, not just in bed."

I know she means that, and her statement emboldens me. I want to do this sexual move even more now, though only with her. "This is called the helicopter. Not sure why, since it doesn't involve rotors and won't lift us off the bed."

"Who cares why it's called that. Just do it, Kendall, please."

"Roll onto your stomach and spread your legs."

Once she's done that, I move onto all fours over her with my head facing her feet. She watches me while I crawl forward until my head is below her feet. Then I clasp my cock with one hand while I shimmy backward to carefully push my length inside her opening until I'm fully seated. Now my head is between her feet. Rachelle sets her hands on my ankles while I begin to thrust in slow motion, triggering her G-spot with every stroke in a manner that regular sex can't achieve. Whilst I fuck her, I clasp her toes with my hands and lavish kisses over her soles and ankles, flicking my tongue out to tease the most sensitive areas. When I simultaneously tickle her toes and tease the soft spot on the inside of her ankle, she cries out and sinks her nails into my ankles.

"Oh, God, Kendall, don't stop. Do that other thing, please, I'm begging you."

I know precisely what she means, and I begin to rotate my hips and push inside her harder and more deeply. She moans, the sound rough and husky, filled with unquenched hunger. I shift my hips until I've spread her folds, though I can't see what I've done. But I do feel it, and the sharp cry that bursts out of her assures me that her clit is rubbing against the bedding in a way that will heighten her need to come.

On that day four months ago, when I had employed this unusual position with her, I'd learned one vital fact about how to make her come. Now, I employ that knowledge again.

I suck on her big toe and push backward into her as hard and deep as possible.

And she comes. Her climax makes her entire body go rigid briefly, then the waves of her orgasm grip me while she cries out. I can't hold off any longer. The pressure in my cock is too intense, and I can barely breathe. So, I give in and let go. Electric spasms rack my cock, and I throw my head back to shout so loudly that my voice echoes through the large suite and probably out into the living room too. It feels so fucking incredible that I need four more thrusts to finish myself off.

Then I collapse onto the mattress with Rachelle's feet bracketing my head.

Neither of us seems capable of moving. We're both struggling to catch our breath, and my heart still pounds like a jackhammer. Once I can inhale and exhale in a somewhat normal manner, I rise to my knees and waddle about until I can lie down alongside her. She snuggles up to me, her smile serenely satisfied.

I brush my lips over hers. "Was it my imagination, or did that maneuver make us both come harder this time?"

"You are not hallucinating. Having this whole big bed as our canvas, we kicked it up several notches on the steamy scale."

"And on the orgasm scale."

Her lips gradually slide into a sly smile. "Oh, yeah, we rocked the orgasms. Got any other wild ideas?"

I focus on her belly, drawing swirling circles on her skin with one finger. "I have many ideas, though I haven't tried most of them. Other women balked at the more unusual positions. But you never balk at anything I want to try, and I love that about you."

She brushes her lips over mine. "You are my favorite person in the whole world. And I would love to try more unusual positions with you. Not right now, though. The helicopter was so intense that I need a break before we try something else. We aren't far from the Thames. Are you up for a walk along the river?"

"Yes, I would love that. It's convenient that Hugh's flat is near the river. We only need to take a short walk to reach it, then we can follow the river trail."

The idea of taking a romantic walk with Rachelle sounds like heaven to me. Am I falling for her? We've only been together for less than three weeks, yet I already know I could fall for her.

But will she still want me once I tell her about my past?

Chapter Thirteen

Rachelle

Our walk along the Thames is magical, but not strictly because of the scenery. I love holding hands with Kendall, chatting with Kendall, doing pretty much anything with Kendall. I might be falling for him, but it's too early to worry about the consequences of that. For now, I simply want to relish this time with him. After the unbelievably hot sex we enjoyed earlier, I need some time to wind down and relax. Conversation is a great way to do that.

But Kendall beats me to it. "You mentioned that your parents are divorced and your mother is French. She lives in France now, doesn't she?"

"Yeah, she does. Mom has lived there ever since the divorce."

"Have you seen much of her over the years?"

I see a bench up ahead and lead us toward it. Once we've sat down, I tell him what he wants to know. "You remember I told you that my parents got divorced during my junior year of college. Mom moved away as soon as the divorce was settled, and that only took a few months. Mom went back to France. She did talk to me about the situation before she left, and I understood her reasoning. Didn't agree with it, but I understood."

"So, have you been in touch with her?"

"We didn't speak for a long time—because I was angry with her for walking away from me and Dad." I gaze out at the river for a moment before I share the rest. "Five years later, I finally realized I didn't want to spend the rest of my life blaming Mom for breaking up our family. I wanted to have a relationship with her. We're both adults, after all, and Dad made his peace with Mom way before I did. She and I became texting buddies and eventually phone buddies. We're friends now, and I'm really glad for that."

"Have you seen your mother in person?"

"Oh, yeah. Mom flies to Missouri every Christmas and for my birthday. At least once a year, she pays for me to go to France."

"It's wonderful that your family has been so mature about the situation. Do you have any siblings?"

"Nope. Maybe that's why it was easier for me to forgive Mom. I don't have a sibling, so there are no sides to take." I turn toward him slightly. "What about your family? You haven't said much about them."

He winces and scratches the back of his neck. "I apologize for being cagey about my family. I mentioned to you once that Mum and Dad disapproved of my former career. They were horrified, actually. But I failed to mention that I also have a brother and a sister, both younger than I am, who also were disgraced because of what I once did for a living. Our mates and neighbors were scandalized, and we were ostracized for a time."

"That's awful, Kendall." I realize exactly what he just said, and that leads to another question. "You said your brother and sister *were* ashamed of you. Do you mean that they aren't anymore?"

"You are the cleverest person I've ever met. You are correct in assuming that Spencer and Bindy recovered from the shock, eventually. We get together whenever I come to London on Sommerleigh business. That means lunch at a pub, usually."

"That's great. I'm so glad you have a good relationship with your siblings."

He eyes me sideways. "Aren't you going to ask about my parents?"

"If you want to tell me, I'll listen. Your decision."

"Mum and Dad forgave me, and we do all right as long as no one mentions my previous career. I see them once a year on my annual holiday, and occasionally in between those times."

I can't explain why, but hearing that he isn't estranged from his family anymore gives me a sense of relief. "You don't need to tell me everything about your past, but maybe you could answer one more question for me."

"All right."

"Where does your family live? I mean, in what part of London?"

"Tottenham. It's a working-class neighborhood. I was born and raised there."

I hesitate while I try to decide how much I should ask of him today. But I decide to try for one more question. "Did you go to college?"

"No. I couldn't afford it. Besides, my father had suffered a work accident and couldn't get back to his job for nearly a year. To help my family, I took on the only job I could get and lied to my family about what I was doing."

"Are you ready to tell me about that job yet?"

"I would prefer not to."

Well, we have been together for less than three weeks. I suppose it was too much to expect him to tell me everything now. Maybe after the Halloween party, he'll feel more open to sharing his secret. I can't imagine it will be a bad secret. He thinks it is, but I've gotten to know him, and he's not the kind of man who would do anything illegal or immoral. I've gotten a bit more information from him, and that's enough for today.

We walk back to the flat and don't discuss our pasts anymore.

The last week of our holiday in London flies by, and before I know it, we have only two days left. On our second-to-last day, we drive to the South Bank, which Kendall tells me is a touristy part of London. We go there strictly so he can buy fancy food stuff at the Borough Market. He has become obsessed with cooking the perfect gourmet meal for our last night in the city, and I'm happy to oblige him. The man could get a job as a chef at a swanky restaurant because he's just that good at cooking.

As we're entering the market, I mention my opinion that he's the best chef in the world and should switch careers.

"I have no interest in working at or owning a restaurant," he assures me. "I'm quite happy with my job at Sommerleigh House."

"Have you ever cooked for the Parrishes?"

"No. Sommerleigh has an excellent cook. And I prefer to make meals for the people I care about the most, such as the woman in my life."

"Oh, and what's her name?"

He slaps my ass. "Cheeky chit."

The Borough Market is amazing. Every stall we visit boasts incredible options like fruits and vegetables, cheesemongers, butchers, fishmongers, bakeries, and even spices and nuts. Kendall selects a wide variety of items, but he refuses to explain to me what he plans on cooking up for us with all those gourmet goodies. That man knows how to keep a secret, but I'd already figured that out.

Everywhere we go, we see Halloween decorations, Halloween costumes in shop windows, and signs advertising Halloween-themed events. I'd almost forgotten that the spooky holiday is coming up. I've been so wrapped up in spending time with Kendall that everything else faded into the background.

Since it's mid-afternoon, Kendall suggests we visit a bakery, so we'll have something to snack on when we get home. That means we wind up buying gourmet brownies, and of course, they smell so good that I can't wait until we get back to the flat before I eat one. And another one. And another. Kendall snatches the box away from me before I can eat any more of them.

"You won't be hungry for dinner, Rachelle, if you gorge yourself on desserts."

"Why did you only eat half of a brownie? They're too yummy to have just a sliver."

He continues driving with one hand so he can reach into the box and pull out a brownie. Then he stuffs the whole thing into his mouth and chews it up. Bits of brownie dribble from his lips.

I lean over and lick them off.

Kendall swallows his treat and wipes his mouth with the cuff of his shirt. "You shouldn't lick my lips that way, darling, unless you want me to drag you into the backseat again."

"You really don't understand how to discourage me. Your threat isn't a threat at all. I would love to get naked in the backseat with you."

"Let's not do that right now. I'm saving my energy for tonight."

"Good plan."

Before heading back to the flat, we stop at a costume shop to browse the selections for Halloween attire. It's strictly window shopping, since Kendall tells me that the Parrishes prefer to provide costumes for the guests at their Halloween soiree. Still, it's a hoot to try on a Catwoman mask, or in Kendall's case, a Dracula cape. Damn, he looks dashing as all get-out in that thing. All he needs is a pair of plastic fangs, and I'll let him bite my neck anytime.

Honestly, I'd let him do that without the fake fangs.

My British Dracula pulls me close and whispers into my ear, "I would love to nibble on your neck, but more than anything, I want to sink my fangs into the warm, slippery flesh of your clitoris."

Despite the plastic fangs hampering his speech, he still makes that statement sound so damn hot that my breath catches.

I boost myself up on my tiptoes to whisper into his ear, "Buy the fangs. Might come in handy tonight."

He rushes over to the checkout counter and buys the fangs.

Our goodbye-to-London dinner is the most scrumptious food I've ever eaten. Instead of having sex afterward, though, we opt for cuddling on the sofa to watch a silly rom-com. We both heckle the movie, which is a lot more fun than just watching it. The dialogue is goofy, anyway. It deserves to be mocked.

For the past three nights, before we go to bed, Kendall has read excerpts from the steamy parts of Owen's romance novel to me. I don't really pay attention to the story. Kendall's voice captivates me, and of course, we always "shag" afterward. But tonight, he doesn't read to me. We both just want to enjoy lying in bed together, all cozy and warm under the sheets.

Hugh had called this morning to tell us our "chauffeur" would pick us up at six p.m. tomorrow evening for our journey back to Sommerleigh. That gives us the better part of tomorrow to enjoy one last touristy day in London. I'm positive our assigned driver will turn out to be Arthur.

In the morning, we enjoy a breakfast whipped up by me, which Kendall insists is the most delicious food ever created. He's full of "rubbish," and I tell him that flat-out, but he doesn't care. I don't mind his hyperbole, not when he's grinning at me and calling me "darling" again, like he had last night. I love it when he says that.

Now, it's time to visit Mayfair.

I've heard the name before, but I have no idea what the Mayfair area is like except that I'm pretty sure it's super-swanky. Kendall confirms my belief. He takes my hand as we amble down the streets and gives me historical information about various locations—like Down Street Station, which is a "tube" station. That means a subway in American. We could go on a tour of the historic station where Winston Churchill took shelter during the World War II blitz, but it doesn't sound fun enough to waste some of our remaining day on exploring the interior.

We agree to make our tour of Mayfair strictly for gazing at the architecture. So, we walk past St. James Palace and Brown Hart Gardens, getting a good workout along the way. We even see one of those red telephone boxes, and Kendall insists on taking "piccies" of me standing both inside and outside the booth. Then I cajole him into doing the same. We've been taking pictures of each other and the sights we've seen during our whole three weeks in the city. I must have hundreds of photos on my phone just from this vacation.

But my favorite picture was snapped by a fellow tourist. It shows me and Kendall embracing and smiling at the camera. We look as happy as I feel all the time when I'm with him.

Kendall suggested we should take a little detour and visit Leicester Square so I can see the most famous statue in London, according to Kendall. It's called the Eros Statue, but it doesn't depict that god. Naturally, I'm confused.

"Perhaps I can clear up the mystery for you," Kendall says. "The statue actually shows the god Anteros. He was the god of selfless love, whereas Eros represented erotic love. The statue is officially called the Shaftesbury Memorial Fountain in honor of the seventh Earl of Shaftesbury."

"How interesting. There really should be a combined god for selfless and erotic love. The two should go together, don't you think?"

"That's an excellent idea. Let's travel back in time to tell the ancient Greeks about that. I'm sure they'll be happy to change the pantheon."

I poke him in the side. "Now who's being cheeky?"

He grins. "Guilty as charged."

My gaze returns to the statue. "The winged god looks like he's pulling a bowstring back so he can fire off an arrow. So, why does he have a bow but not an arrow?"

"No one really knows, though there are theories."

"Ooh, I love a good mystery. Why don't we try to come up with our own crazy conspiracy theories about it? That sounds like fun, doesn't it?"

He chuckles. "With you, everything sounds like fun."

That might be the best compliment I've ever received.

I cajole Kendall into posing for a picture with Anteros, and he snaps one of me too. Then we cuddle up under the statue for a joint selfie. Just as he hits the button on my phone, he lunges his head to smash a kiss on my cheek. When I look at the picture he took, I look stunned—because he surprised me. Oddly, that image is my favorite. It seems appropriate that the man who took my breath away the moment we met should be the one who takes a picture like that of the two of us.

But I do need to mete out a little payback for that stunt. So, I grab Kendall's hand, tugging until he starts walking with me, and then I drag him around and around the statue while he makes the cutest pseudo-annoyed face. I might be thirty-nine, but that doesn't mean I can't still do silly things. I'm a children's author and illustrator, after all. Silly is my middle name.

Just as we've crossed the Piccadilly Circus road junction, on our way back to the Jaguar, Kendall abruptly halts. He stares wide-eyed at…something. Is it the building in front of us? The traffic lights? Neither seems plausible.

"Kendall, what's wrong?"

I suddenly notice a man who just emerged from the shadows of an archway on the front of a fancy old building. The guy is jogging toward us. "Kendall, do you know that man?"

He doesn't respond or move even one finger.

I shake him, and finally, he swivels his gaze toward me. But he immediately swerves his attention back to the man heading for us.

What in the world is going on?

Chapter Fourteen

Kendall

The stranger jogs directly up to me and lightly punches my chest. "Kenny, mate, it's been forever. Where ya been? I almost didn't recognize you, with your flash clothes and a hot girlfriend. Don't I get an introduction?"

I can do nothing but gawp at the man. I vaguely recall his name, and he seems faintly familiar, but my vocal cords refuse to function. When I had glanced at Rachelle, she had seemed completely flummoxed. I don't blame her for that reaction.

The bloke lightly punches me again, this time with both hands. "Come on, mate, you've got to remember. It's me, Robbie Marsden aka Stroker Chase."

My lips begin to move, though I still cannot produce anything resembling a syllable, much less a word. Sentences are so far beyond my reach that they might be on another planet.

Rachelle slips her hand into mine, lacing our fingers. "Hi there, I'm a friend of Kendall. And you are Robbie Marsden. Are you a writer? That's a strange pen name if you are an author."

"Pen name?" Robbie says with a chuckle. Then he pulls his chin back and scrunches his eyebrows at me. "You have no idea, do you?"

"No idea about what?" Rachelle turns her gaze to me. "What's going on here, Kendall?"

Robbie seems rather wounded by my refusal to acknowledge him. *Bloody hell*. I hadn't recognized him at first, since he's considerably older than when I knew him. Now that the memory has come back to me, what's the point in pretending I have no idea who the bloke is? I sigh and smile tightly. "It's good to see you again, Robbie. What sort of work are you doing these days?"

He stares at me with utter bafflement. "What do you mean? I'm the headliner at Bodacious Nights. After you left, Candace promoted me to lead dancer."

Rachelle gawps at me as if she's never seen me before. "You're a dancer? Like in a ballet?"

My former coworker laughs with more vigor than seems necessary. "Ballet? Is that what American birds call that sort of thing?"

I need to explain all of this to Rachelle, but not in front of Robbie. He's a decent bloke, but he always loved the job more than I ever did. And I'd rather discuss this with only the woman beside me. But I speak to Robbie. "I'm glad to hear you're doing well, but I'm out of that lifestyle. Afraid we don't have much in common these days. Cheers."

With my hand tightly clamped around Rachelle's, I virtually drag her down the street until we're out of sight of the spot where we'd encountered Robbie. Oddly, I don't feel as much shame or embarrassment as I would have expected. Perhaps that has something to do with Rachelle. Over the past three weeks, I've realized that she will accept me no matter what I do for a living or what I've done in my previous life.

And it's time for me to tell her everything. Before the Halloween bash. Before the insanity begins in earnest. Before the American Wives Club shifts into high gear.

"Would you mind if we go back to the flat now?" I ask her. "The conversation we need to have will be easier in private."

"Your sudden desire to open up happened because of that guy Robbie."

"That was the push I needed to share everything with you. No more secrets."

She grins as I open the car door for her and offer my hand to help her get inside the Jaguar. She keeps grinning while I climb in and we start down the road. In fact, she doesn't stop smiling even when we walk into the flat and settle onto the sofa.

I shake my head at her, amused by her excitement. "If you're hoping I'm actually a space alien or a Bond-style spy, you'll be disappointed."

"Nothing about you could ever disappoint me." She wriggles until she's sitting cross-legged, facing me. "Go on, start talking. I'm so excited to hear the truth."

"The bloke we met at Piccadilly Circus, Robbie Marsden… We used to work together at a night club." I suddenly feel as if the cushion beneath my arse is made of jagged pebbles. Shifting my arse this way and that doesn't help. "It was a specific type of night club."

"What type?"

"A male revue."

Her blank expression either means she doesn't understand or she's stunned beyond the ability to speak.

I rub my eyes, wincing harder than ever before. "I was the headliner at a club where men dance in an erotic manner."

She bites down on her lips while her shoulders quiver with contained laughter. Then she stops trying to contain it. "You are so cute when you're pussyfooting around an issue. Come on, spit it out. I know what you're talking about, but you need to say it out loud. Get it off your chest."

"I just did get it off my chest. Were you not listening?"

"You really aren't going to say the words, are you? Okay, I'll do it." She leans toward me. "You were a stripper."

"I prefer the term male revue dancer."

"But you took your clothes off. That's called stripping."

Have those pebbles under my arse mutated into shards of broken glass? It feels that way.

Rachelle doesn't seem at all fazed by my confession. "Did you go all the way? Total nudity?"

"No, I never did that. My, ah, private parts were covered by a G-string. Robbie was much raunchier than I was and often took everything off."

"His stripper name was Stroker Chase, right? He mentioned that name, but I wasn't sure why until now."

The only response I can manage is to nod once.

"Will you tell me your stripper name?"

She deserves to know everything, so I might as well get on with it. I clear my throat. "I was Rod Thruster, Maverick of the Wild West End, King of the Pelvic Thrusts. That's how the emcee always announced me, though it's a bloody ridiculous name."

"You were the headliner. That's what you said." When I nod again, she...kisses my cheek. "Thank you for telling me all of that. Did you become a stripper because your family needed the money? You mentioned once that your parents couldn't accept what you did for a living."

"That is the reason I was estranged from my family for a time, though it was mostly because of my shame, not theirs. I tried to hide what I was doing for as long as possible, but then everything fell apart when a hen party showed up at Bodacious Nights. That's the club where I was the lead dancer."

"Can't deny I like the name of that club. It doesn't sound very British, though."

"The woman who owned the club, Candace Weaver, is American. She came up with the name." I set my feet on the coffee table and sink into the sofa. "The hen party I mentioned included a woman I recognized—because she is my sister."

Rachelle pinches up her entire face. "Ouch. What happened when she realized the hot guy ripping his shirt off was you?"

"She screamed—with horror, not excitement. Then she muscled her way through the throng of ravenous women, trying to reach the main doors, I'm sure. But she could only get as far as the women's loo."

"Then what happened?"

"My routine had just ended, so I put on a dressing gown and rushed to find Bindy. She was in the loo, crying. I tried to explain, but she was horrified to find out what I'd been doing. The next day, I told the rest of the family. My brother, Spencer, took the news only marginally better than Bindy had. Mum and Dad didn't know what to say. I left and never went back."

"Your family didn't understand."

"No, they were confused and shocked. I had to give up my flat and move into a boarding house. I'd quit my job, you see. Then

I spent a few years doing odd jobs and moving from one place to another until I finally saw an advert on a notice board. It was the Parrishes, looking for a butler."

"And you've been hiding out at Sommerleigh ever since."

"Not hiding, not precisely. I simply didn't want to face my family. I had humiliated them enough for one lifetime." I reel my thoughts back in time to the moment when I had first met the Parrish family. "I have no idea what the elder Lord and Lady Sommerleigh saw in me that made them want to hire me, but I will always be grateful they took that chance."

"I'm glad they did too. I might never have met you otherwise."

"Don't you want to tell me I should go see my family?"

She climbs onto my lap, straddling me. "That's your decision to make."

"Why are you on top of me?"

"Because I can't seduce you into doing what I want unless I'm holding you down with my body." She slides forward until her hips meet mine. "I'd love for you to show me your stuff."

"What stuff?"

"Your stripper routine."

I choke on my own saliva. "What? You can't want to see that. Besides, I don't have the proper kit. The sort of dancing I did requires special clothing that can be easily torn off."

"Give it a try, please. If you don't show me, then I'll have to imagine it myself, and I'll probably fantasize about something much raunchier than what you actually did."

"So, this is blackmail."

Rachelle leans her beautiful body into me, crushing her tits to my chest. "Think of it as making me happy. Then I'll make you happy afterward."

"All right. You have seduced me, darling."

She lifts her head, her face alight with excitement. "You'll strip for me?"

"Yes, I will." I rise with her in my arms, then walk round the sofa to the open area between the living room and kitchen island. I set her down. "You will sit on a stool while I prepare. You want the full Bodacious Nights experience, yes?"

She nods vigorously.

"Then sit on a stool and close your eyes."

Rachelle obeys my command. "This is so exciting."

"You've seen me naked many times. Why should a striptease be so thrilling for you?"

"Don't know. It just is." She catches her bottom lip between her teeth and releases it slowly. "Well, it probably has something to do with your stripper name."

"Ah, I see. Since I don't have an emcee, I'll narrate the show myself."

"Oh, good. I love your voice."

"The striptease won't be as polished as what I used to do because of the, ah, wardrobe issues."

Rachelle has kept her eyes closed just as I told her to do. What a wonderful woman she is.

"Hurry it up, would you, Kendall? The anticipation is killing me."

"I need to go into the bedroom first so I can gather the appropriate items." I jog into the large suite and hunt about until I have everything. Then I return to the living room. But before I allow her to open her eyes, I set one item on the bar. "Do not touch this even after you've opened your eyes. Understand?"

She salutes. "Yes, sir, Mr. Thruster, sir."

Oddly, I don't mind that she used my stripper pseudonym. Robbie had announced his stage name. And I had grimaced hard enough that I must have popped a vein or two, simply because I was afraid he might blurt out my stage name too. But I would love to hear Rachelle use that pseudonym.

I pick up her index finger and set the tip on the required spot. "When I tell you to, open your eyes and push this button."

"What is it for?"

"You'll find out when I'm ready to show you."

I move onto the appropriate spot. "Open your eyes and push that button."

Rachelle's eyes fly open, and she punches the button on the boombox without even glancing at it. Her gaze is nailed to me. "You're wearing a suit. That's not what I expected."

"I had to improvise. Now, listen and watch." I take a deep breath and blow it out. "Welcome to Bodacious Nights, the hottest high-class male revue in London. I'll be your emcee and dancer this evening—Rod Thruster, Maverick of the Wild West End, King of the Pelvic Thrusts. And for tonight, I'll break every rule of male revue clubs." I wink. "For your eyes only, darling."

She feigns a swoon and fans her face with one hand.

As the opening music gives way to the main event, I begin to move my hips in time with the thumping bass and rhythmic electric guitars, and the sharp sound of the snares adds that extra bit of flair. I chose the most sensual yet uptempo song I could think of for my first number.

I thrust my hips forward in sharp movements.

"Woo!" Rachelle shouts. "Give it to me, baby!"

Lodging my hands on my hips, I shove my thumbs inside my waistband and do a sideways sliding move I'd learned from Robbie Marsden. I make it my own by pumping my hips and rolling my torso in a snakelike manner.

Time to strip.

As soon as the first song ends, the next begins. I sway my hips from side to side, bending my knees and straightening them, repeatedly, in time with the music. I slowly undo my tie, but I don't remove it, not yet. Then I turn away from Rachelle and slowly push my suit jacket off my shoulders while keeping up the hip movements.

I glance over my shoulder and wink at Rachelle.

She pretends to faint, though she only sags against the bar. "You're killing me, Rod. Show me some skin before I pass out."

"The customer is always right."

I whip off the jacket just as another sensual song begins. I toss the jacket away and spread my feet on the floor, gradually bending my legs while undulating my hips in time with the hot beat.

When I glance back at Rachelle, she dips her fingers into a glass of water and splashes her face. I had left a glass on the counter for her, though I hadn't guessed she would use it to cool her libido.

Now, it's time for the big finish. I chose a faster paced song to make this bit even more exciting and erotic. I spin round and rip my shirt open wide. Buttons tick on the floor. I toss the shirt away, though I still wear the tie. As the sensual beat and the suggestive lyrics take hold of me, I stop thinking and just do it. Unhooking my belt, I fling that toward Rachelle. She catches it. I drop to my knees and pump my hips as I undo the button on my trousers and drag the zipper down inch by inch.

Then I leap to my feet and kick the trousers away.

When Rachelle sees I have no undergarments on, her jaw literally drops. "So, this is what you meant when you talked about that casual dance training with your dad. It paid off later because it got you the stripper job."

"That's right."

For the final flourish, I stalk up to Rachelle and pull her into my body. For a moment, we simply stand here like this while her breaths grow more and more labored and my cock feels ready to explode. Then I thrust my hips in a sensual, rolling movement, over and over until she's panting for me.

I release her and step backward a few paces. I'm breathing just has heavily as she is. "How did you like your first male revue experience?"

"Holy fucking hell on flaming wheels, Kendall."

"Does that mean you liked it?"

"No." She marches up to me and strips her blouse off. "It means fuck me now, Rod Thruster, Maverick of the Wild West End." She rips open the clasps on her front-close bra. "Does this visual aid make the point?"

"Yes, loud and clear."

Chapter Fifteen

Rachelle

Oh. My. God. I have never gotten this hot for a man before, but watching Kendall strip had been the most erotic and arousing thing I've ever seen. I'm so wet that my panties are actually soaked. That's not hyperbole. One guy I dated did a striptease for me, but it was downright tame in comparison to what Kendall just showed me. It was more than a performance. He gave me goosebumps, amped up my libido to a dangerously high level, and showed me a side of him I will need to see again sometime.

I ditch my bra and lean into him, pressing my breasts to his muscles. "Let's get it on right here on the floor."

His lips gradually slide into an expression I've never seen from him before—a lascivious grin imbued with fiery male hunger.

But we don't get the chance to do what I suggested.

The distinctive chunk of a door lock being disengaged makes us both swivel our heads toward the front door. We glance at each other, eyes wide.

"Oh, bollocks," Kendall says exactly when I say, "Oh, shit."

From the other side of the door, I hear Avery's voice. "Hugh, don't just barge in. It's rude. You lent this flat to Kendall, and you wouldn't want to accidentally walk in on him changing clothes. I wouldn't mind, but—"

"Avery, darling, could you please not discuss another man's nudity?"

Yep, Lord and Lady Sommerleigh are here—several hours early.

Kendall scrambles to get his pants and shirt on, settling for not tucking the shirt in since we're pressed for time. I can't resurrect my bra, and I can't blame Kendall for that. I went nuts and ripped it open myself.

I sprint for the bedroom to grab another shirt, finding and pulling it on in record time. That means I reach the front door only a minute or two after Kendall opened it. Lord and Lady Sommerleigh seem rather flummoxed by his state of disarray. The immaculate butler has mussed hair, wrinkled clothes, and no shoes.

Avery elbows Hugh in the side. "I told you we should have hung out in a café for a while instead of showing up early."

Hugh grins. "Yes, they've clearly been shagging relentlessly." He punches Kendall's arm. "Good on ya, mate."

"You have no idea what we might have done," Kendall points out. "Your suppositions are bloody annoying."

"Must have been one cracking shag all right. I've never seen you so feisty and insolent. You haven't even called me Lord Sommerleigh."

"Bugger off, Hugh."

Kendall slams the door shut.

My jaw falls open. "You were so rude to your employers."

"Sorry. But I just don't give a toss about manners right now." He drags me into his body. "Need to fuck you, Rachelle, immediately."

"As much as I'd love that, Hugh and Avery are waiting out in the hall. They lent you this flat and gave you a three-week holiday. You can't just blow them off." I clasp his face with both hands. "You'll hate yourself later if you keep acting like a prick."

He closes his eyes, pulls in a big breath, and exhales it slowly. The lustful tension evaporates, and his muscles slacken. "You're right. Forgive me, love?"

"Of course. It's my fault, anyway. I talked you into doing that intensely hot striptease for me."

"Perhaps I'll do that for you again sometime—when we're completely alone."

"It's a date."

He opens the door in a more leisurely manner. "I apologize, Lord Sommerleigh, Lady Sommerleigh. My behavior a few moments ago was inexcusable. Please accept my apology."

"Can't accept it," Hugh says. "You didn't do anything wrong. We're the wankers who turned up without notice earlier than expected."

Avery puckers her lips at Hugh. "We? Speak for yourself, Lord Steamy."

He bows deeply. "Please forgive me, my lady. I am the sole wanker in this situation."

"Much better." She grins and winks at me. "That's how a viscountess tames her husband."

I don't want to tame Kendall, though maybe I would like it if he's naked and I'm the cowgirl roping the horny bull.

As we walk over to the bar, Kendall doesn't get the slightest bit anxious when Hugh and Avery notice the boom box and the fact that Kendall's shoes and tie are strewn across the floor. Hugh's brows lift the barest bit, that's all. Then he smirks at Kendall, who narrows his gaze on the viscount.

We gather up our luggage and follow Lord and Lady Sommerleigh out to a limousine. It looks like the same one we rode in before, but all limos look pretty much the same to me—unless it's one of those custom models. Arthur is in the driver's seat, as usual.

During our trip back to Sommerleigh, we stop often at petrol stations along the way. Avery will whisper something to Hugh, then he will nod and tell Arthur that "the lady of the manor needs a 'pit stop,' so find a petrol station." Minutes later, Arthur pulls off the road, and Avery rushes into the restroom. After the tenth stop, I get curious.

"Are you okay, Avery?" I ask. "You seem like you're having a problem."

"Oh, no. There's no problem." She and Hugh look at each other, then engage in a brief, hushed conversation. She faces me and Kendall and smiles. "Hugh and I have decided to share our news with you. Derek and Rosalyn already know, which means Diana knows too."

"What about Arthur?" Hugh asks. "He's right behind us."

The driver coughs loudly. "Should I roll up the partition?"

Hugh and Avery exchange another look, and she smiles at our driver. "No need for that. You're family, Arthur."

The man seems surprised by that statement. "Thank you, Mrs. Nibs."

She smiles and shakes her head, then turns to us. "My frequent need for pee breaks has a legitimate reason. We found out last week that I'm pregnant."

"That's wonderful," I say. "Congratulations."

Kendall grins and leans over to slap Hugh's arm. "Good show, mate. Before long, we'll have a little Lord Steamy running round the estate, or perhaps a Lady Steamy."

"Let's hope my child doesn't come with a prepackaged nickname. I want our son or daughter to choose their own path."

"Of course. But as your honorary brother, I reserve the right to spoil your children."

"I wouldn't want it any other way."

Hugh shoos his wife away, urging her to move further down the bench seat. Then he opens up a panel in the center of the seat, which turns out to be a cooler. He brings out a bottle of sparkling white grape juice. "Let's all celebrate the newest member of the Parrish family."

Lord Sommerleigh finds four glasses and hands them out to all of us, including Arthur. Then he pours the sparkling juice. We all clink our glasses and congratulate the parents-to-be.

"Have you thought of any names yet?" I ask. "Must be so exciting to have a baby on the way."

Avery glances at her husband, her expression filled with love. "It is exciting. And wonderful. And a little scary. We don't know yet if we're having a boy or a girl, but we've already started coming up with a list of candidates for our baby's name."

Hugh glances at me. "You're a children's author. Do you have any name suggestions?"

"I'm an illustrator and an author. If you want a picture book about your child, give me a call."

"What a brilliant idea," Arthur says. "You can call the book *His Nibs, Mrs. Nibs, and Little Nibs Go to Town*."

"That's quite a mouthful. But I love your enthusiasm."

Hugh groans with sarcastic annoyance. "Arthur, let's not name the child any version of the term Nibs. All right?"

"Whatever you say, Lord Sommerleigh."

"If it's a boy, our top candidate is Lawrence, not Nibs."

By the time we reach Sommerleigh, we've stopped at least a dozen times to let Avery use the restroom. None of us care that the journey took longer than normal. We're so happy for Hugh and Avery. After everything Lord Steamy went through last year, it's amazing how much his life has changed.

My life has changed radically too, all because of the butler.

The second we step out of the limo, a crowd rushes out of the house to swarm the driveway and the steps. Rosalyn manages to disperse the throng so she can reach us, though all she does is gaze imperiously at the people gathered out here. Everyone minds the Dowager Lady Sommerleigh.

Dominic and Chelsea, along with Owen and Poppy, squeeze through the crowd to reach us.

Kendall stares at Poppy. "Who's minding the bookshop?"

Poppy kisses Kendall's cheek. "Don't worry, pet. Owen found a highly qualified person to take over for the long weekend. We couldn't miss the Sommerleigh Halloween bash."

"Had to literally drag her out of the shop," Owen says. "Poppy kind of turns into a control freak whenever she has to hand the shop's reins over to someone else. You did a fantastic job, Kendall, but we need you here for the party. Pardon me, the bash."

Kendall's brows furrow. "Who is this mysterious, qualified person?"

"Audrey Corbyn."

My honey's eyes widen to the point of almost bulging. "What? An international bestselling author who has sold millions of books offered to mind a little bookshop for the weekend?"

"Yeah. Audrey and I are, uh, old friends."

Poppy snorts, trying not to laugh. "He means that he had a fling with her once upon a time. They're just mates now."

Someone whistles with such piercing volume that I just stop myself from covering my ears. The person who made that sound suddenly has everyone's attention, and we all swerve our attention to him. "We were meant to wait in the ballroom, not out here. Get your arses into the house now."

I sidle closer to Kendall. "Who is that blond guy?"

"Chance Dixon. He's the eldest of the Dixon brothers, but he lives in America with his wife Elena. They've come for the Halloween bash, presumably."

"Wow, I didn't realize it was going to be such a huge event. Do most of these people have kids?"

"Yes, they do."

I rise onto my tiptoes to peer at the crowd. "How will everyone and their kids fit inside a ballroom? Is the one at Sommerleigh gigantic?"

"No. Sommerleigh is a Victorian house with an average-size ballroom. I can't fathom how they think everyone and their children will fit in that space."

Hugh chuckles. "No one has told you, have they?"

I set my heels down again and turn to Hugh. "Did who tell us what? I'm totally confused."

"We told you this year's Halloween soiree would be transformed into a bash for the ages. That means no children. The grandparents will mind the kiddies while the rest of us enjoy a bacchanalia."

"Baka-what? If this is turning into some kind of Roman debauchery with orgies, then—"

"Relax, Rachelle. We are not vulgar Romans. This is an adults-only bash, but we will not tolerate any offensive behavior."

Dominic and Chelsea have just reached us, and the former cricket star has kept his arm around his wife as if he thinks she might get swept away by the crowd. "No profane behavior? I was led to believe we could have fun at the big do. If you're banning all cursing and lewd jokes, I don't know if I want to attend."

"Swear all you like," Hugh assures Dominic. "I was merely allaying Rachelle's fears that we might be luring her into Satanic sex rites."

"Damn, no Satanic sex?" The man who spoke those words has pushed his way through the throng to reach us. He sounds American. "Here I was hoping I could do some naughty spells to make Diana do whatever I want in bed. Oh, wait, she already does that. Never mind."

Hugh sighs with immense sarcasm. "Derek, you American heathen, how many times have I told you? If you want to cast demonic spells on your wife, do it when I'm nowhere in the vicinity."

These people are so strange, but I'm starting to like their twisted sense of humor. It's all in good fun. I can tell that by their expressions and tone of voice.

Derek surveys the crowd and shakes his head. "Somebody needs to get this under control."

"You want to do it," Hugh says. "So go on, Sheriff Hahn, corral them. That's the American word for it, isn't it?"

"Everything you know about America came from B-movie cowboys." Derek faces the myriad people gathered here. Then he shoves two fingers into his mouth and whistles even louder than Chance Dixon had. Jeez, everybody here loves to make ear-piercing whistles. "Listen up, everybody! Lord Steamy is about to blow a gasket because you guys aren't following the plan. So, get your asses in gear and head for the ballroom. Stragglers will be imprisoned in the Sommerleigh Dungeon."

Hugh throws his head back and growls. "Derek, you know nothing about subtlety, do you?"

"Subtle wasn't getting the job done."

We wait while the crowd troops into the house, then Kendall takes my hand to lead me inside. Hugh, Avery, and a few others accompany us through the foyer and down the long hallway until we reach the grand staircase. That's what I've decided to call it, though I kind of doubt the Parrishes would ever use that term. I don't get the chance to ask because Kendall is half dragging me up the stairs while the others struggle along behind us.

Is he nervous about this Halloween party? Why would he be?

Before I can ask the question, we've entered the ballroom. Arthur and a few others approach Kendall, including Mildred the cook, Beatrice the maid, and Simon the horticulturist. Gee, I thought it was a garden out there, not a horticultural exhibit.

"About time you got here," Mildred says. "Lord and Lady Sommerleigh took your itinerary and ripped it to shreds. Can't believe half the things they put on the list."

"What new list?" Kendall asks. "I thought it was only minor alterations. That's what Lady Sommerleigh told me."

Arthur chuckles. "And you believed His and Hers Nibs? They put one over on you, mate. The sedate soiree you planned has become a bash for the ages."

"I'm bloody sick of hearing that term. What in the world does it mean?"

The screeching of a microphone draws everyone's attention to the stage set up at the far end of the ballroom. Hugh stands atop it, frowning as he fiddles with the microphone. After one more sharp screech, he seems to have gotten the hang of it. "Ladies and gents, welcome to the first-ever adults-only Halloween Bash hosted here at Sommerleigh House. Tomorrow night, the true orgy—ah, *revelry* shall begin."

"Come off it, Hugh," Dominic hollers. "No one believes you want a Roman orgy."

Hugh ignores his friend. "We have chosen fancy dress costumes for you. Each guest will wear an ensemble that's both appropriate for Halloween and highlights their personal style."

Do I have a personal style? Don't think so. Besides, these people don't know me well enough to choose a costume that suits me.

Hugh continues with his speech. "You will receive your fancy dress costumes tomorrow, shortly before the bash begins. Please do not get pissed before the big event actually commences. Exercise restraint. You don't want to fade away before the main event."

I edge closer to Kendall and whisper out of the corner of my mouth, "Is he telling us not to pee on the floor?"

Kendall's lips twitch, and he wipes a hand over his face while his shoulders quiver with contained laughter. "No, pet, he's telling us not to get drunk. 'Pissed' is the British word for that."

"Oh, good. If we had incontinent people here, I might just run all the way back to London."

Hugh raises his arms. "And now, ladies and gents, please come up here to the table on the dais behind me and find your room assignments and your assigned time to pick up your fancy dress costume tomorrow. We're chuffed that all of you chose to celebrate the wickedest holiday with us."

Wickedest? Oh, yeah, I'm getting a sneaking suspicion about the kind of outfits Hugh and Avery have chosen.

Tomorrow night, I'll find out if I'm right.

Chapter Sixteen

Kendall

I drop onto the bed backward, close my eyes, and sigh with a depth of relief I have never experienced before in my entire life. How can anyone be this knackered and stay awake? My body seems to weigh a metric ton. Despite my exhaustion, I can't deny the truth. I've never been this happy in all my life, and it has very little to do with the impending Halloween bash. It's entirely because of one woman.

I peel my lids open to watch Rachelle stripping. All my contentment originates with her.

But she is not doing the sort of striptease I used to get paid to perform. She's simply undressing and changing into the skimpy lace nightie she had worn every night in the London flat. I can just see the outlines of her nipples through that fabric, but I get a splendid view of her arse when she turns away from me while sliding the nightie down over her body.

I wish I had the energy to shag her, but I don't. Surprisingly, I'd much rather curl up in bed with her and fall asleep.

We have been given the largest guest room in the house, with a spacious walk-in closet, two dressing tables, a shower stall, and a bathtub. I know this room well, having lived at Sommerleigh House for most of my adult life. I know all the rooms, including the viscount's suite.

Rachelle settles in on the bed while I quickly get rid of my clothing. She watches me with a sort of appreciation I've come to know well. She loves admiring my body, even more so since I performed my striptease for her. I love the way she watches me. It makes me randy, but I'm too knackered to make love to her. I doubt she wants to do that either. Today has been a whirlwind.

She's wearing a nightie. I don't own any sleepwear. She already knows that, so I climb onto the bed and pull the covers over us. I instinctively roll onto my side and drape an arm over her belly. She rolls over to mold her backside to my front. While Rachelle's body slackens, I gently reach over her body to turn off the bedside lamp. Only the glow of the full moon provides illumination.

"Is this the room you always sleep in?" she asks. "You don't seem like the kind of man who wants a fancy bedroom when your fellow employees have smaller rooms. Or do all of them have big rooms too?"

"No. The staff, including me, have average-size quarters, though our rooms include showers instead of bathtubs."

"Hugh and Avery gave you a special suite?"

"It would seem so. Not sure how I feel about being in the second-largest suite at Sommerleigh House while my coworkers will remain in their usual quarters."

She rolls over to face me. "You are not a traitor for sleeping in here with me. I might not know the other staff members well, but I have noticed that they love you. They admire you too."

"Admire me? Why? I'm a butler, nothing more."

"Bullshit, Kendall. During our last pit stop at a petrol station, I went into the restroom with Avery." Rachelle lays a hand on my chest, splaying her fingers. "Avery told me that a butler does a heck of a lot more than just answer the phone and greet guests. You're a household manager. You keep track of the Sommerleigh budget as well as order supplies and keep the pantry stocked up, not to mention checking that everything in this house is in good working order. You also book appointments for the Parrishes and the staff, everything from doctor's visits to airline flights. And that's the tip of the iceberg."

Why on earth would Lady Sommerleigh tell her all of that?

"Face it," Rachelle says. "You are the heart and soul of Sommerleigh. Don't take my word for it. Hugh and Avery both know it's true. So do Arthur and the other employees."

"You've spoken to all of them?"

"Not the whole staff. But Arthur vouched for what Avery had said. He told me that you are the one holding this place together."

My throat has gone thick. I can't speak because I can't believe what Rachelle has told me. She wouldn't lie, of course. But I had no idea how my fellow employees feel about me or what the Parrishes think of me either. I've done my job, nothing more, nothing less. Yet they praise me for it. I might never have known how they feel if I hadn't met Rachelle. Everything has changed because of her.

I turn onto my back, holding on to Rachelle so she ends up sprawled half on top of me. Her hair tickles my chin. The sweet, natural scent of her envelops me. "Let's go to sleep, love. It's been a long day. Long but good."

She makes a sleepy moan of agreement.

With Rachelle in my arms, I fall asleep swiftly. When I rouse in the morning, the sun is shining and birds are singing, just like every day at Sommerleigh. But this morning is different. I have Rachelle here with me, yes. But it's more than that. My life has changed drastically, and I don't mind one bit.

Rachelle stretches and moans with satisfaction, though she hasn't opened her eyes yet. Her mouth stretches into the sweetest, most contented smile I've ever seen. I smile too, and the expression probably matches hers. I have never been this contented before in all my life.

But a thread of anxiety sifts through me. Tonight is the Halloween bash. What insanity will these people conjure up for us?

Rachelle opens her eyes and tickles my lips with her fingers. "You're worrying again. Because of the Halloween party, I assume."

"What else? I don't like surprises."

She laughs softly. "No kidding. You ran away when you saw me again in Poppy's bookshop."

"That wasn't my finest moment. I was stunned, that's all. Couldn't believe a woman like you would fly across an ocean to find me."

Someone raps on the door.

"Piss off," I shout. "We're still asleep."

Rachelle lifts her brows, her lips twitching upward a touch.

Yes, I am lying outright and in the most unbelievable manner.

"Asleep?" Dominic says. "I knocked, and you told me to piss off. Are you sleepwalking, Kendall? Must be sleep-speaking too, eh?"

"Go away."

"Not until I've delivered my message. Breakfast will be served in fifteen minutes. There, I've done my job. Better shag Rachelle quickly or you'll be late, and you know how Hugh gets when his meal isn't on time. He turns into a werewolf."

Hugh wouldn't give a toss about his meal being late. Dominic is just trying to harass me. And Lord Sommerleigh is absolutely not a werewolf.

Since he doesn't speak again, I assume he has left the vicinity. I sit up and stretch. "Time to get up, Rachelle. We've been summoned to breakfast."

"Great. I'm so hungry."

We shower and dress with just enough time left to walk downstairs rather than jogging. As we enter the dining room hand in hand, the other couples in attendance glance our way and smile knowingly. I swear every one of them does that. It's bloody annoying. When I pull a chair out for Rachelle and push it in once she's sat down, the others all grin at me.

I ignore them.

Not all the guests who have come here for the Halloween bash are in the dining room. The space isn't large enough for everyone. As I take my seat beside Rachelle, I ask, "Where is the rest of the horde? Have you tossed them out onto the lawn? The grass isn't as thick this time of the year, so they won't have much to eat."

The room goes silent. Everyone stares at me.

I glance round the room. "What have I done?"

Hugh clears his throat. "You made a joke. That's what you've done, Kendall. But I think I can speak for everyone in this room—except for Rachelle, presumably—when I say that your good humor this morning is unprecedented."

"Sorry. I didn't mean to offend anyone."

"Offend?" Hugh says with a laugh. "You misunderstand. We are not annoyed by your behavior. We think it's bloody fantastic."

The others express their agreement in a chorus of overlapping voices.

For once, I do not blush when I receive a compliment. I am overwhelmed by the sentiments everyone expresses, but I accept all of it calmly. As I glance round the table, I see Hugh, Avery, and

Rosalyn, naturally. But I also see Diana and Derek Hahn, Chance and Elena Dixon, Dominic and Chelsea Rigby, and also Bennett Montague and his wife, Samantha.

The former crown prince now lives in the little village of Cockshire here in England, though he grew up on the island nation of Mithoria. For Ben and Sam to be here... *Oh, bollocks.* That means this will be an insane Halloween bash, even more so than I had anticipated. Cockshire is five hours away from Sommerleigh, after all. No one would travel that far simply to play dress-up for a few hours in the ballroom.

I lean toward Rachelle and whisper, "I'm getting a bad feeling about this bash. It might turn into something...risqué."

She whispers too. "The former stripper is worried about risqué behavior?"

A loud throat-clearing interrupts our sotto voce discussion.

Rachelle and I both veer our gazes to the man who made that sound.

"I can read lips," Ben Montague says. "My best mate at school was hearing impaired, and he taught me to read lips. I learned sign language from him too."

Hugh sits forward in his chair at the head of the table, his eyes alight with mischief. "What did Kendall and Rachelle say, Ben?"

"Ah, it's not my place to reveal that information. I spoke up only to let Kendall and Rachelle know that someone else might also have known what they were saying."

"I doubt anyone in this group aside from you can lip read."

Rosalyn, who sits beside me, gives my hand a squeeze. "Don't feel pressured to share your private conversation. My son can be rather obnoxious about such things."

The twinkle in her eye assures me she's having me on—about Hugh being obnoxious. But she was quite serious about the other bit.

Here with my mates, on this Halloween day, I suddenly realize I don't want to keep secrets anymore. It's time for me to tell them everything. I glance at Rachelle, and she nods. That's all the assurance I need.

I push my chair back and stand up. Then I tap my fork on my water glass to get everyone's attention. "I have an announcement to make."

No one speaks, though everyone watches me.

"You have all wondered about my past, and I'm about to explain in full." I resist the urge to glance at Rachelle again. This is something I need to do on my own. "Rosalyn already knows my secret, but it's time I told all of you. Before I came to Sommerleigh, I worked as a dancer in a male revue club."

Most of the people in this dining room seem rather confused. I need to clear up my meaning.

I take a breath and do it. "For those of you who don't know what a male revue is, it means that I was a stripper at a club called Bodacious Nights."

Hugh gawps at me with his jaw slack, but beside him, Avery seems tickled pink by the news.

Rosalyn stretches a hand out to hook her finger under Hugh's chin and push it upward. "Close your mouth, dear. A fly might wander in there."

When she pulls her hand away, Hugh keeps his mouth closed but continues gawping at me as if I've grown three extra heads and insect antennae. He jumps out of his chair. "Are you having me on?"

"No. It's all true."

"But you—" He shakes his head slowly. "You would never even remove your suit jacket on a warm day. When I invited you to go to Nick and Siobhan's house for a pool party, you absolutely refused because you didn't want to expose your chest. You are the most anti-nudity person I've ever met."

"I was ashamed of my past for a long time. But Rachelle has shown me that I have no reason to feel shame. I did what I had to do to help my family."

Hugh seems so genuinely shocked and confused that I feel as if I need to... I don't know. Comfort him, I suppose. He is like a brother to me, after all, and I've just shattered all his preconceptions about me.

I walk round to the end of the table and clamp a hand on his shoulder. "I'm sorry to disappoint you. My past isn't something most people would want to hear. I'm a butler, after all. That sort is meant to be upstanding and proper."

Hugh's expression abruptly shifts, turning from shock to wry humor in a way only he could pull off. And he smiles in his usual sly manner. "Kendall, you're talking to Lord Steamy. I once played shinty in the nude, and I attended a nude wedding. I, of all people, have no right to criticize your former career. And honestly, it does explain a lot about you."

"You don't want to sack me?"

He laughs so boisterously that his eyes begin to water. "No, you fool, I would never sack the man who's like a brother to me."

"That reminds me of something else I need to confess. I have a brother, and a sister too. Every time you send me to London on errands, I meet up with Spencer and Bindy for lunch."

"You have siblings? For pity's sake, man, why did you keep all of this a secret for seventeen bloody years?"

I shrug. "Because I didn't want to be cast out. My parents didn't react well when they found out I was an exotic dancer at a raunchy revue club. I can't blame them."

Hugh studies me for a moment, tipping his head slightly to the side and narrowing his gaze. "Do you visit your parents? Is that what you do on your holidays?"

"Yes. Our relationship is still somewhat strained, but we get on all right."

He shakes his head again, even more slowly. "Unbelievable. Is your butler routine an act?"

"Of course not. Taking a job here at Sommerleigh was the best thing that ever happened to me. I love this family, and I would never do anything to hurt you, Rosalyn, Avery, or the staff."

Rosalyn rises. "I think the ladies and I need to have a private conference about tonight's festivities. You gents need some time to digest all that Kendall has told you. Come, ladies, we have so much to do."

Hugh squints at his mother. "Why is this the first I've heard of a special ladies' conference?"

"Because I just announced it, that's way. Do try to keep up, Hugh, darling."

The women file out of the room, chattering and laughing all the while.

Dominic leaps out of his chair. "Since the ladies have gone, we might as well start the festivities early. That means a round of cricket."

"Why not football instead?" Derek asks. "I mean the real version that's played in America."

"Could we not argue about which version of football is legitimate? Besides, I said cricket. That's a completely different sport." Dominic looks at me. "Do you play cricket, Kendall?"

"No."

"Would you like to learn? It's not that difficult."

I suspect he's trying to create a bonding experience for me, so that the other men in attendance can get to know me better. I appreciate that, but it sounds like absolutely no fun at all. Cricket is a violent sport. I've never even tried to play the game. What if I get whacked in the head with a cricket ball?

No, I will not be a coward. I used to strip for a living, while women stuffed pound notes into my G-string and some even tried to climb on stage to sexually harass me. That means I can handle anything. Cricket has nothing on a male revue.

"All right," I say. "Let's play cricket."

Dominic slugs me in the gut, but not hard. "Don't forget to bring your groin pads."

Chapter Seventeen

Rachelle

Rosalyn has claimed my hand and refuses to let go even as we exit through the solarium doors and out onto the patio. She keeps smirking at me too, with a deviousness that does not bode well. What is she up to? The Dowager Lady Sommerleigh seems to love mischief. When I asked her where we're going and why we need to go there, she just smiled and winked.

All the women in attendance at Sommerleigh, including the ones I haven't met yet, have gathered on the lawn for a confab. Most of us sit down on the grass, but the pregnant ones prefer chairs. They stay on the tiled patio.

Even Rosalyn sits on the lawn—in a very ladylike pose, naturally.

I'm sitting cross-legged beside her. She's wearing a dress, so I understand why Rosalyn doesn't adopt a cross-legged position too.

Then she pulls a little bell out of her pocket and jingles it. "Quiet, ladies, please. The conference is about to begin."

Everyone shuts up.

Rosalyn sets her bell on the grass. "Now, I know we had previously agreed upon the events for tonight's bash, but circumstances have changed. We've just been gifted with a smashing opportunity, and we can't possibly ignore it."

Elena, wife of Chance Dixon, raises her hand. "Um, what are you talking about, Rosalyn?"

"The fancy dress, dear. I'm proposing that we change the style."

I bite the inside of my lip for about two and half seconds, then I can't hold back anymore. "What style? I thought we just wore costumes and danced."

"Oh, dear child, it is far more than that. Hugh, Avery, and I agreed that the bash needs to be something spectacular this year, something for adults only. But Kendall's confession has given me a brilliant idea. Shall I elaborate?"

Every head nods, including mine.

She leans forward and says in a pseudo-whisper, "Listen closely, darlings. We have the chance to turn a simple fancy dress ball into a night we will all remember for the rest of our lives."

I slant toward Rosalyn. "What is the plan?"

"A secret, dear. That's what it is." She glances at her watch. "My accomplice should be arriving at any moment."

I open my mouth to speak again, but Rosalyn abruptly shoves two fingers into her mouth and whistles so loudly that my ears hurt.

When she sees my wincing expression, she grins. "Derek Hahn taught me how to whistle that way. He's a treasure, and quite the hottie too."

I can't deny I'm surprised that an elegant lady like Rosalyn would use the word hottie to describe a man. Then again, I have heard her call Derek "the American stallion" and refer to Dominic as "the Dom I'd love to shag."

Okay, yeah, it's no surprise at all.

Arthur trots out of the solarium, heading straight for us, clearly having responded to Rosalyn's eardrum-piercing whistle. When he reaches her, he bows deeply. "What can I do for you Mrs. Nibs Senior?"

"How many times have I asked you to call me Rosalyn?"

"Rather often, I'd say."

She grasps his chin and pulls down until his eyes are aligned with hers. "Then start calling me Rosalyn, please."

"All right, ma'am." He straightens. "What can I do for you, Roz?"

"You are such a cheeky sod. Fortunately, I love that in a man." She holds out her hand to him. "Help me up, dear. Has our last group of guests arrived yet?"

"Oh, yes, Roz. They're in the sitting room."

Arthur helps her get onto her feet, which is made a little more difficult by her long dress. It's beautiful and suits her perfectly, but the designer didn't account for a lawn party when they designed the garment. Once she's on her feet, she brushes off the fluttery folds of her dress.

Then she holds her hands out to two of us. "Rachelle, Avery, would you please come with me, my darlings? I need your input on the special project."

We both say yes, of course, and rise to join her.

"For the rest of you darlings," Rosalyn says, "I invite you to go to the solarium for a refreshing bit of rhubarb cordial. That's a nonalcoholic drink, for those of you are or might be in the family way. There will be snacks too."

Arthur leads the way as Rosalyn hooks one of her arms around mine and curls the other around Avery's arm. We walk swiftly across the patio and through the solarium, straight down the hall until we reach the sitting room. Arthur opens the door for us, shutting it behind himself once we're inside the room.

Three people wait for us, two women and one man.

Rosalyn guides me and Avery to the sofa, where we sit down on either side of her. A younger man and woman sit in adjoining chairs. The other woman is older and regally sits in a high-back chair near the windows, across from the younger couple.

Who are these people?

Rosalyn smiles at the newcomers. "I'm so pleased to have you three here for the big bash, as my darling daughter-in-law calls it. Avery and Rachelle, allow me to introduce our guests." She waves toward the younger couple. "You've met Chance and Dane Dixon today. The gorgeous young man joining us is Reese Dixon, their younger brother. And the bombshell beside him is Arden, Reese's wife. As for the blonde beauty across from them, this is Celeste Arnaud. She not only is Arden's grandmother but also a business tycoon and the billionaire founder of Bonsoir Beauty."

I can't contain my surprise. "Bonsoir? My mom gave me some of their makeup and face cream for my birthday last year. It's amazing."

Celeste smiles at me. "Thank you, dear. I'm so glad you enjoy our products. My grandson-in-law is the marketing genius of our company, and his older brother Dane used to work for me too. Dane created some of our bestselling vibrators. But that sweet boy has now returned to his mechanical engineering roots."

Reese gets up and approaches the sofa, offering me his hand. "A pleasure to meet you, Rachelle. It's about bloody time Kendall found the right woman, and one who's beautiful and sexy. What a lucky bloke."

"It's wonderful to meet you, Reese. Your brothers are fantastic, so I never had any doubts that you would be too."

He grins and glances at Rosalyn. "I love this girl. It's a good thing you mobilized the American Wives Club, or else Kendall might've hidden in the broom closet for the rest of his life." He kisses my hand. "See you later, Rachelle. I've got to go show my brothers how cricket should really be played."

Reese saunters out the door.

Arden laughs. "You'll get used to Reese. He's a sweetie underneath all that brash attitude."

Rosalyn pats my thigh. "Now that Arden and Celeste are here and you've met them, it's time to join the others in the dining room. We need to have a meeting about the special event Celeste and I discussed on the phone earlier."

Celeste rises. "You are absolutely right, Rosalyn. Let's see how many younger women we can shock with our idea."

I flick my gaze back and forth between the two older women. "Why do you want to shock us?"

Rosalyn winks. "You'll see, dear."

She and Celeste lead the way as we exit the sitting room. Avery and I exchange confused looks, but Arden seems to be in on the secret. Her knowing smile and twinkling eyes tell me I'm right. Once we reach the dining room, I realize it's completely packed.

As we stop just outside the doorway, I ask, "How can we have a meeting if we're all jammed in like sardines? Besides, there are too many of us here to have a genuine conversation."

"We are not here to converse," Celeste says. "We're here to share our idea and let everyone vote yea or nay. It's quite simple."

I must seem dubious because Rosalyn wraps an arm around me. "Relax, pet. We have the situation well under control. But you are correct. This room doesn't seem large enough. We should relocate to the ballroom. Don't you agree, Celeste?"

"Yes, I do see your point." She shoves two fingers into her mouth and whistles loudly. I guess the whistling thing is contagious. Once everyone inside the room has stopped talking and turned to face the doorway, Celeste addresses the group. "Ladies, we don't want you to be stuffed into this cramped dining room any longer. Please come with us to the ballroom, where we can convene a meeting of the American Wives Club in comfort."

Celeste and Rosalyn start walking down the hall again. Avery, Arden, and I follow them with the rest of the women trailing after us. I glance back. Holy cow, there are more women here at Sommerleigh than I realized.

The tables for last night's dinner are still arrayed inside the ballroom, so all the ladies begin to form small groups at each table. Rosalyn and Celeste invite me, Avery, and Arden to join them at the table they've chosen, which lies at the other end of the large space. I wind up sitting between Celeste and Rosalyn, with Arden and Avery at either side of the older ladies. Our table is large enough for a few more people, so Rosalyn invites the wives of Chance and Dane Dixon to join us. Rika and Elena sit directly across from me.

Celeste shouts for another woman to join us, and I get to meet Maddie Hunter. She's married to Richard Hunter, one of the Hunter twins. I'd already heard that Richard owns a publishing company and that Maddie is a freelance disease detective, which means she searches for the causes of disease outbreaks. My job seems frivolous by comparison. So, when Maddie asks me what I do for a living, I hesitate to respond.

"Don't be shy, Rachelle," Maddie says. "We won't make fun of you if your job is something weird. I mean, Dane used to make sex toys. Trust me, we're all open-minded here."

"My job isn't weird. It's just not as glamorous as Celeste's or as important as yours."

Rosalyn slings an arm around my shoulders and gives me a light squeeze. "It's all right, dear, you can tell us. If Kendall could share his previous occupation, then you have no reason to feel ashamed of what you do."

She's right, and I'm being silly. "I write and illustrate children's books."

The ladies at this table fall silent for several seconds. Then Rosalyn hugs me. "That's wonderful, Rachelle. I would love to see some of your work. Do you write under a pseudonym or your real name?"

"I use a pseudonym. Buckholtz isn't the most appealing last name."

"May I ask what your author name is?"

"Everly Harmon."

Arden perks up. "Wow, that's a fantastic pen name. I need to look up your books."

"They're just silly things for kids."

She leans closer and whispers into my ear, "This is top secret, but I'm pregnant."

Elena shakes her head at Arden. Her lips tick upward. "Honey, you need to learn what whispering really is. We all heard what you said."

"Oh. Well, then, I don't need to keep it a secret anymore. Reese and I will finally have a baby of our own after nearly three years of putting it off because we were traveling for his job." She looks at me. "So you see, I do need your books, Rachelle."

Rika's brows shoot up. "Is there an epidemic of pregnant women here?"

"No, silly," Arden says. "But when you have this many women in one place, and when they're all married to super-horny men, you're bound to have more of us who are preggers."

Rosalyn and Celeste whisper something to each other, then both women push their chairs back and rise.

"Listen up, ladies," Celeste calls out to the crowd. "Rosalyn and I have come up with a fantastic idea for a special event during the Halloween bash. It will be daring and unprecedented here at Sommerleigh. Rosalyn, would you like to share our idea?"

"Of course." Rosalyn smiles with impish delight. "All right, ladies. Are you ready for this..."

Chapter Eighteen

Kendall

"That was a good game, eh, mate?" Reese Dixon says as we and several other men walk up the patio steps, heading into Sommerleigh House. "I mean, Dane cocked it up when he tried to hit Hugh's fast ball, but nobody can blame him. He's an engineer, not an athlete. Now Dom knows how to hit that ball and send it flying all the way to Leeds. But me? I've got the charm, youth, and speed that all of you decrepit blokes can't match."

Dane Dixon gives his brother a playful shove. "Shut your bloody mouth, Reese. Only Arden wants to hear your lies about how incredible you are. Besides, you couldn't even hit the ball."

Hugh jogs up beside me just as we walk through the solarium doors. He grips my shoulder so firmly that it almost hurts. "You should've tried being the striker, Kendall. This was a match strictly for fun, so you didn't need to worry about looking like a ruddy moron."

"I don't enjoy sports. Taking the wicketkeeper position was all right, but I find cricket to be rather boring."

"Boring? You are off your trolley. Cricket is fast-paced and delivers all the thrills."

Nick Hunter glances over his shoulder at us. "I prefer my thrills in the bedroom, Hugh. Cricket is a pleasant distraction, but women love a good full-body massage."

Hugh aims a sardonic look at Nick. "Are you sure your day spa isn't actually a prostitution ring? Having sex workers in your spa would be a violation of the law, even if prostitution is legal in other contexts."

Reese groans miserably. "Could we not talk about boring rubbish like the law? This is meant to be a fun Halloween weekend. You lot are turning it into a day at school."

"Is that why you couldn't concentrate on the game?" Chance Dixon asks his youngest brother. "You thought it was a maths test. We all know you can't count to five on one hand."

Despite the fact that I like all these gents, and I did enjoy serving as wicketkeeper, I've grown tired of the sarcasm and camaraderie. I want to find Rachelle and take a nap with her in our suite. Why didn't I think about shagging her? Because I'm too bloody knackered after taking part in a sporting event. I will definitely need a good long lie-down or I'll never stay awake for the big bash.

Hugh slows down to walk beside me as we pass through the solarium and out into the hall. The others have moved ahead of us, far enough away that we can talk without needing to whisper.

"Tell me the truth, Kendall. Are you wishing you'd stayed in the house to be with Rachelle?"

"Yes. Aren't you thinking the same thing about Avery?"

"Of course I am. But Avery is my wife. You and Rachelle have only known each other for a few weeks, and I have no frame of reference for your kind of relationship."

"Because you used to shag lots of birds, but you only ever had one relationship—and it's with Avery."

He slugs my arm playfully. "You're a clever sod."

"It doesn't take any particular intelligence to figure that out. I'm sure even Reese Dixon could do that."

Hugh tucks his chin, eying me with a touch of surprise. "Were you just employing sarcasm? I'm not used to you behaving like a normal bloke instead of the Sommerleigh automaton."

"I am not a machine. Being good at my job does not mean I have no soul."

Lord Sommerleigh wraps an arm around my neck. "You've always been a brother to me, but now we can finally talk to each other like mates. It's about bloody time."

I peer down the hall where the other blokes are. "Do we have free time now? Or has the American Wives Club organized some other sort of outdoor event for us?"

"Not sure. Once Callum and Kate arrive, we might do something else."

"Please don't tell me there will be caber tossing."

"Why are you so averse to sports?" Hugh punches me lightly in the gut, and he keeps hold of my neck. "Ah, but you like other sorts of physical activity. Performing a striptease must be hard work."

"Could we not discuss my former career?"

"I thought you were no longer embarrassed about it."

A sigh rushes out of me. "That doesn't mean I want to talk about it incessantly."

The men further down the hall have stopped and now form a sort of congealed mass of muscular bodies. Hugh drags me down the hall with his arm still constraining me, until we reach the throng.

Hugh releases me and glances about as if he's expecting something. "Where are Mum and Avery? Their group chat can't possibly have gone on for this long."

Near the far end of the hall, a door bursts open and bodies pour out and into the foyer, a horde of woman that descends upon us. Every married woman grabs her husband, and every married man seems utterly confused. I might be single, but I also have no idea what is going on now. I can say only that the group chat is indeed over.

Avery leaps on Hugh, forcing him to wrap his arms around her waist to keep her from tumbling to the floor. She showers kisses over his face while smiling in a decidedly carnal manner. Poor Hugh can't seem to catch his breath. Then Avery at last sets her feet down and gives her husband a bit of air. As I survey the crowd, I notice that all the women seem unusually...ardent.

What on earth did they talk about for two hours? What could make them behave in this way?

Rachelle finally reaches me and throws her arms round my waist as she hoists herself onto her tiptoes to plant a firm kiss on my lips. "Mm, I missed you, Kendall."

"You saw me two hours ago."

"But I didn't get to..." She places her lips over my ear. "Didn't get to smack a big wet one on you before you took off."

Hugh clears his throat deliberately. "Kendall, perhaps you and Rachelle should go into your suite to—"

"No, Hugh, they can't do that," Avery declares. "You boys have something to do to help us get ready for the Halloween bash. It's mandatory."

Celeste Arnaud and Rosalyn approach us. I've met Celeste many times when she visited Sommerleigh, but I had no idea she would be here for the Halloween soiree. The woman is in her seventies, much older than Rosalyn, but I have no doubts she can and will remain at tonight's big do until everyone else has left. She loves a good party.

Grey and Jessica Dixon squeeze through the crowd to reach us.

I gawp at them, simply because I hadn't known they were coming to this weekend bacchanalia.

Jessica kisses my cheek. "It's so good to see you again, Kendall. When Rosalyn called yesterday to invite us to this big bash, we couldn't resist. It sounds like a hoot and a half."

Grey kisses his wife's forehead. "Jess, you were begging me to come to this party. How could I say no to the love of my life?" He veers his gaze to me, and he waggles his eyebrows. "Finally found the right girl, eh? Good for you, mate. About bloody time."

Why does everyone say that to me? *About bloody time.*

All right, maybe I haven't dated that often. And maybe I hadn't tried very hard to show women that I'm not just a dull, uptight butler. I had quick shags with girls, nothing more. But still, I wish everyone would cease and desist pointing out those facts by incessantly stating that it's about bloody time.

Poppy and Owen approach us next. I say "us" because Rachelle refuses to peel her body away from mine. Can't say I tried very hard to dissuade her. Perhaps I didn't actually try at all. I love to have her body pasted to mine.

We all get a surprise when another woman follows Poppy and Owen over to our little group. I don't recognize this woman, but the others clearly do. Well, other than Rachelle.

Owen waves toward the other woman. "I think you and Rachelle are the only ones who don't know about this girl. She's my ex-wife, Naomi Hansen, and she's American like me. Naomi tried to get between me and Poppy last spring, but it didn't work out for her. She's reformed her ways, and after spending a few months on Sir Dexter Armstrong-Hill's private island, she feels much better—about herself and about making amends. The three of us have made peace. We're friends now."

Poppy rolls her eyes at Owen. "Honestly, love, you didn't need to tell them the entire story right now. Naomi just arrived from Manchester half an hour ago. Let her decompress."

"I don't need any decompression," Naomi says. "I've been working as a manager at a cinema, not running an international corporation. But getting away from my job for a couple of days sounds fantastic. Thank you all for letting me join the party."

I sidle up to Owen. "In your book, you claimed a man can get an erection instantly, but that's rubbish."

"Yeah, I know. But readers love that stuff."

"I see. Did you model your hero on me?"

He gives me an enigmatic smile and walks away.

Celeste throws her arms up and whistles. Once everyone has stopped talking and turns in this direction, she lowers her arms. "Listen up, gentlemen. The Sommerleigh Halloween Bash committee has discussed tonight's festivities and decided to add another one. We will require the participation of eight men, but first, we will need to examine all of you to determine who is best suited to this event."

Best suited? I don't understand what she means.

Celeste isn't done speaking. "First, we will need to inspect all of you and see you in action. Kendall will help us with this task."

"What? I don't want to inspect anyone. What on earth is this about?"

"You'll find out once we're in the ballroom." She waves dismissively. "Ladies, you have the rest of the afternoon to do whatever you like. Do not under any circumstances try to peek inside the ballroom. We will have Derek Hahn drag you away and lock you inside the sitting room if you do."

The thunderous snarling of a motorcycle erupts outside.

Hugh bursts into a fit of excitement, grinning and laughing as he hauls Avery out into the foyer. He flings the doors open and throws his arms wide. "Callum and Kate are here! Now the bash will really begin!"

Rosalyn shoos everyone out of the way so that she might drag me and Rachelle into the foyer. Through the open front doors, I can see the big, loud machine that has just pulled up in the circular drive. The man and woman seated astride the Harley remove their helmets and grin.

Callum MacTaggart leaps off the bike and plucks his wife off it too, setting her down. She waves him away. He races up the steps to suffocate Hugh with a boisterous hug, after which he punches his best mate in the gut. Not with any real force, naturally.

Hugh grins. "It's been too bloody long, Callum. Can't get your wife to leave Scotland, eh?"

"Kate was ready to go the moment you rang us with the invitation to the Halloween bash. But I had to finish a carpentry job first."

"Doesn't matter. You're here now." Hugh seizes Kate in a firm hug the moment she reaches the top step. He kisses her cheek, then gestures toward me and Rachelle. "You'll never believe it, but Kendall finally got himself a proper girlfriend. This is Rachelle Buckholtz, and she's an American like you."

Callum and Kate both approach us to offer their congratulations on our new relationship. Then Hugh gets that devious glint in his eyes, the one I know all too well, and I realize he has something up his well-tailored sleeve.

Hugh pushes between Kate and Callum, sliding an arm across each of their shoulders. "We have even bigger news on the Kendall front. He finally revealed his secret past to everyone, and you'll never guess what he used to do for a living."

Callum squints as if he's giving serious consideration to the question of my former career. "Was he a drag queen?"

"No, but you're close." Hugh smirks. "Kendall used to be the lead dancer at a male revue club called Bodacious Nights."

Callum's face goes blank briefly, then he bursts out laughing. "That's brilliant. The butler was a stripper. No offense, laddie, but I had you pegged for a serial killer or maybe a librarian. This is so much better."

Kate eyes me with a new appreciation. "Wow, I never would have guessed. Did you take it all off? Or did you keep a G-string on?"

"I stripped down to a G-string."

Hugh's annoying smirk deepens. "Why don't you share your stripper name with Kate and Callum?"

"You think I'll be embarrassed, you wanker, but I'm not." I face Kate and Callum. "I was known as Rod Thruster, Maverick of the Wild West End, King of the Pelvic Thrusts."

"That's quite a mouthful," Callum says.

"I was normally just called Rod Thruster. But as the headliner, I was given a special, longer introduction by the emcee."

Kate roves her gaze over my entire body. "Gotta say, I'm seeing you in a new light."

Callum slaps a hand over her eyes. "No more gawping, *mo chridhe*."

She pushes his hand away. "I was only window shopping, sweetie."

Celeste appears in the doorway. "Time to go, gentlemen. That includes you, Callum."

Hugh, Callum, and I follow her into the unknown.

Chapter Nineteen

Rachelle

"Now remember, Rachelle dear, do not eat anything before the Halloween bash. You don't want to have a full stomach before you even walk into the ballroom. Don't consume any alcohol either, not until everyone is in there. The surprise we have planned for this evening will be wonderful, I promise you that. And oh, my dear sweet girl, you look absolutely stunning in your fancy dress costume. I knew you would be smashing in it, and that's why I chose it for you."

Rosalyn and I are standing in the foyer, waiting for the rest of the gang to get their outfits on, but in my mind, I keep hearing what she'd told me earlier. Why shouldn't I eat anything? Or have a drink? Not sure. But I'm getting the idea that this party will involve more than showing off our costumes. Rosalyn won't share any details, though. I've asked her twice and got no response.

Well, unless a smug smile counts.

Rosalyn appraises my outfit for the second time tonight. "Oh, my darling girl, you look utterly smashing. The moment Kendall sees you, he will want to whisk you away to your suite and ravish you for hours."

"You don't talk like most women your age that I've met."

"Because I speak the truth? Tosh. I am not eighty years old, and even if I were, I would not become a prude."

"Yeah, I can't imagine you blushing at the thought of two people getting it on."

Rosalyn takes hold of my upper arms and kisses both my cheeks. "I'm so happy that you and Kendall met, or I would never have gotten to know you. Would it be cheeky of me to say I hope you two will get married soon and have lovely little boys and girls?"

A nervous laugh bubbles out of me. "Since you just said it anyway, there's no point in asking if I mind."

She leans in to whisper into my ear, "Perhaps you'll start the process tonight. I was not inflating the truth when I said you look stunning."

I can't deny that the outfit Rosalyn and Celeste chose for me is gorgeous. I'm a witch, but not a *Wizard of Oz* kind. My entire outfit, from head to toe, features shades of green to match my eyes. The silky fabric of my costume is dusted with glittery little sequins, and the sleeveless dress has a plunging neckline as well as a skintight bodice. The hem falls down to my ankles, but a daring slit goes all the way up to my hip. The flowing skirt is almost transparent, though it becomes opaque nearer to my hips. My green shoes glitter too. And yes, I wear a glittery green hat in the typical conical witch style.

I hold up my magic wand. "Am I supposed to cast a spell on Kendall?"

"Oh, my dear, I'm certain you've already done that." She studies my ensemble one more time. "Your smoky eye makeup is the pièce de résistance. I guarantee that Kendall will ravish you all night long, once the bash is over."

"Honestly, Rosalyn, you are the naughtiest aristocrat I've ever met. Well, Hugh is very naughty too. Come to think of it, I've never met any other lords or ladies."

"It's a family trait. You should have heard the things my husband Lawrence used to say. He was a lovable rake, just like Hugh." Rosalyn's humor abruptly vanishes, and she becomes more serious. "We have arranged another surprise, especially for you and Kendall. I hope you two won't be annoyed that we took the liberty."

"Took what liberty? I don't know if I should be offended, since I have no idea what you guys have done."

"You'll see soon enough." Her smile returns, and she gives me a quick, firm hug. "Enjoy the Halloween bash. It will be a once-in-a-lifetime experience."

"I'm sure it'll be loads of fun."

We had all eaten a light snack around five o'clock, so that we would be "ready and raring to go," as Reese Dixon had told us, and we wouldn't be too full to enjoy the food and drinks during the bash. The tactic worked. It's almost eight o'clock, and though I'm not about to keel over, I am getting a touch hungry.

The other ladies rush down the stairs, each wearing a unique, ultra-sexy Halloween costume. Like my outfit, none of theirs are lewd in any way. They're hot but tasteful. The women head for the closed doors of the ballroom to await the big moment when all will be revealed. Only Avery stops to talk to me and Rosalyn.

"Isn't this exciting?" Avery says. "Sommerleigh has never hosted an event quite like this one. I can't believe Kendall agreed to our wild idea."

Yeah, I can't believe it either. But I'm getting a little giddy just thinking about it. What Kendall intends to do just might make me swoon. Not because I'm a wuss. No, it will be from the overwhelming power of sheer lust. Oh yes, Kendall is *that* hot.

"You know what," I say. "Actually, I can believe Kendall would do what we suggested. He's been hiding all that wildness deep inside himself for a long, long time."

Rosalyn nods slowly. "I see your point, dear. And you know him better than anyone, so your opinion matters the most."

The doors to the ballroom swing open, and Hugh hits us with his Lord Steamy grin. "Welcome to the Sommerleigh Halloween Bash, ladies. Your charming rakes await you inside."

Hugh is dressed like a sexy devil, which seems entirely appropriate. He wears black tights and matching boots plus a red vest laced with black leather. Since he has no shirt, the skimpy vest exposes a large part of his chest. He wears a pair of red devil horns, of course, and his arms are fully exposed.

Damn, he has great biceps and pecs.

Hugh secures the open doors to keep them from falling shut again. Then he puffs up his chest and makes an imperious hand gesture. "It's all right, ladies. Feel free to swoon and salivate over Lord Steamy, though tonight I shall be known as Lucifer." He spreads an arm wide, giving us all a clear invitation. "You may now enter the underworld."

"Don't you mean hell?" Celeste calls out. "Lucifer lived there. The underworld is from Greek mythology."

Since she's smirking, it's clear she's just having fun teasing Hugh.

"Call it whatever you like, Celeste." Hugh steps aside, now standing just past the doorway in the hall. "Please, find your assigned tables."

This is it. The wildest Halloween bash I've ever attended is about to begin.

Rosalyn urges me to stand near the wall opposite the ballroom doors, and we simply watch while all the other ladies traipse into the space that has been transformed into a spooky-sexy visual treat. Only once everyone else has found their tables does Rosalyn lead me into the ballroom.

The dim lighting and high-tone Halloween decor make this feel like something special, for sure. But a man approaches me, and suddenly, I can't catch my breath.

"Kendall? Is that really you?"

"Yes, darling, it's me." He smirks. "My fancy dress costume is that good? I thought all the women would appreciate it, but I wasn't completely convinced until you looked at me."

Though I might've participated in planning the special event for this bash, I had no idea what kind of outfit Kendall would wear. Rosalyn and Celeste insisted on choosing it themselves.

I knew Kendall had a great body, but damn, his costume goes so far beyond hot that I can't think of a word that might accurately describe it. "Is that a Roman gladiator outfit?"

"Yes. Though Hugh told me it's a gladiator from a male revue, not a historically accurate version."

"Who cares about historical accuracy."

Kendall's outfit is skimpy, to say the least. Fucking hot would be a better term. Nearly all of his torso is exposed, with only a swathe of leather that wraps around one shoulder and becomes narrower as it dives beneath the opposite arm to join with the leather straps on his upper back. His right arm features one long band of leather that extends down to his fingers while several smaller bands encircle his arms with the last one wrapping around his wrist.

But his kilt… *Holy shit.*

A wide band of leather encircles his hips, riding low, and several narrow straps hang down on the front and back. Does he have any underwear? I kind of doubt it. His costume doesn't leave much room for that. The ensemble is topped off with matching knee-high leather boots and a golden helmet that covers his face down to just above his nose. But I can see his eyes, and their beautiful blue color shimmers every time a muted strobe light passes over us.

"Do you like my fancy dress costume, then?" Kendall asks. "Don't give a toss what anyone else thinks, only you."

"I love your outfit. Even Russell Crowe couldn't look this good in gladiator gear."

Rosalyn and Celeste both skim their gazes over my hot boyfriend, clearly impressed by what an incredibly, unbelievably, mind-blowingly hunky stud he is. Kendall should always dress this way, even while he's performing his butler duties. I never want to see him in anything else.

Okay, that's not really feasible. But it's how I feel. I want to jump him right here in front of everyone.

I shuffle up to him and lay my hands on his bare chest. Then I speak in a hushed voice. "I want you now, Kendall."

His lips curl into a sensual smile. "I want you too. Your clothing is making me dangerously randy. I might throw you down on the nearest table and shag you while everyone watches." He glances around the room, then bows his head to speak directly into my ear. "On second thought, I don't want anyone else to see you in the throes. That pleasure belongs to me alone."

The heat in his voice takes my breath away.

Rosalyn taps my shoulder. "Rachelle, dear, I'm afraid it's time to take your seat at your assigned table. Kendall needs to prepare for the special event that will serve as the opening act for this bash."

Oh, the special event. I can't wait to see it. I might know what it is, but I have no idea how it will unfold. Kendall is solely responsible for orchestrating the show.

Reluctantly, I walk away from Kendall. Rosalyn and Celeste lead me to the area of the ballroom where a stage has been set up, and we sit down at our table where a few other people wait for us. Hugh and Avery are here, of course. One chair remains empty, since it belongs to Kendall.

Hugh rises from his seat. "Time for me to go backstage. Avery, I will see you after the show."

Lord Sommerleigh kisses his wife and leaves. He picks up six other men along the way, who each jump out of their seats and rush to follow Hugh around the back of the stage. Reese Dixon, Dominic Rigby, Derek Hahn, Nick Hunter, Callum MacTaggart, and Bennett Montague will all participate in the big show. Kendall is in charge of the spectacle, so I'm not counting him as one of the guys. He has already disappeared behind the stage, which features lush velvet curtains in a deep scarlet shade and a smooth floor erected specifically for this purpose. I also see spotlights. They hang from the poles that hold up the curtains, and more are positioned around the periphery of the stage itself.

The lights go out.

Everyone stops talking, and I swear the excitement is palpable inside the ballroom as every woman and man seated at the tables awaits the big surprise.

A single spotlight comes on directly above the stage.

Next, the pounding rhythm of electronic music starts up with a beat that's sensual and just irregular enough to heighten the tension.

A solitary figure emerges from the curtains and strides into the soft white glow of the spotlight. Hugh holds a microphone in one hand as he surveys the crowd. "Are you ready for the show?"

Women scream and whoop and make catcalls.

None of that fazes Hugh at all. He smirks and waits for the ladies to get it out of their systems. Once they've calmed down, Hugh smiles like the devil he's dressed as and proclaims, "Let the bacchanalia begin."

More screams. More whoops. More catcalls.

Once again, Hugh waits until the crowd calms down. He raises one arm, waving it up and and down while he speaks. "Let me hear all of you, even the men. Tell me how excited you are for the show to begin!"

If I'd thought these women were going crazy a minute ago, now they are completely out of their minds—but in a good way. Everyone here knows each other and loves each other.

So yeah, let the insanity begin.

I throw my arms up and whoop.

Chapter Twenty

Kendall

Oh dear lord, what have I gotten myself into this time? The crowd, especially the women, seem ready to swarm the stage and consume us. But I know they will behave themselves. The shouting and whooping and such is strictly their way of showing their appreciation for what we are about to give them. They know in general what we'll do, but not the specifics.

Hugh hasn't even officially started the show.

I glance at my mates, the men who are willing to potentially humiliate themselves in the name of entertainment. They *are* my mates. No longer am I the stuffy butler who speaks as little as possible and disappears into the woodwork when I'm not needed.

And I'm about to show everyone who I really am.

I can't resist peeking through the curtains.

The spotlight comes on again, and Hugh stands in the center of the cone of light holding the microphone near his lips. Based on his expression, I know he means to invoke his Lord Steamy persona in all its glory. "Good evening, ladies and gents. I am your emcee for this special, one-night-only show exclusively for all of you lovely people, our closest mates and family." He leans forward a touch and speaks in a deeper, sensual tone. "Tonight, you may call me Lord Lucifer Steamy."

Avery whistles. "You rock, baby!"

"Thank you, darling." Hugh spreads one arm wide. "You are about to be transported to another world where eight of the most attractive and lascivious men you will ever meet shall take you down into Lord Lucifer Steamy's den of iniquity."

I part the curtains surreptitiously, just enough that I can get a sliver of a glimpse of Rachelle. Given the lighting, I can't see much. But since she sits at the table closest to the stage, I can at least tell that she's smiling and clearly enjoying the show so far. Lights come on throughout the ballroom where the tables lie, but they're small bulbs designed to provide low illumination. They won't interfere with the crowd's ability to see the show.

"Let your mind go," Hugh aka Lord Lucifer Steamy purrs to the crowd. "Relax, and allow the fantasy to take hold."

He has modified the speech we had agreed on earlier, but I'm not surprised. It doesn't bother me either. I'd panicked when my itinerary had been changed, but now, I don't give a toss. Let Hugh have his fun.

"The countdown begins now," Hugh says. "Count with me. Ten, nine, eight—"

Everyone ticks off the seconds in unison.

"Seven, six, five, four—"

I back away from the curtains to join my mates, glancing at them over my shoulder. Reese Dixon, Dominic Rigby, Derek Hahn, Nick Hunter, Callum MacTaggart, and Bennett Montague await my signal. They know what to do, and if they should cock anything up, no one will care.

"Three, two, one—Liftoff!"

As the spotlight is doused, Hugh hurries back behind the curtain. The sudden loss of the spotlight will have given him the few seconds of lead time needed to retreat back here with the rest of us.

The music halts briefly, then fires up in earnest with a deep, throbbing beat and instrumentation designed to enhance the sex appeal of the song.

Hugh sets the microphone in its stand. No one will be able to see him back here while the rest of us do our parts. He can remain out of sight while narrating the show. "Welcome, ladies and gents, to the wickedest haunt in England! Eight devils in disguise will seduce you with their skill, athleticism, and enthusiasm. Chance, Dane, shut the doors now!"

I hear the ballroom doors slam shut.

Hugh's voice grows deeper and more devilish. "Now you belong to us, here at the club we call Lord Lucifer Steamy's Wicked Bash!"

Women scream. I know those ladies, and I can't believe they're so excited when they have no idea what is coming. I feel the way I used to back when I'd been a dancer at Bodacious Nights, and the mood of the crowd infects me just as much as it did back then. I'm ready for this.

But I'm not first in the parade of fearless blokes.

"And now, show your love for our first performer—Rock Harder, the Young Stud, also known as…Reese Dixon!"

Naturally, he drags out every syllable of Reese's stripper name and his real name, strictly for effect. It works. Even the men are shouting their support for their mate. And I can hear Arden Dixon, Reese's wife, screaming louder than anyone else. I know it's her because she shouts, "Go, Reese baby, go!"

Hugh and I pull the curtains back just enough to let Reese walk through them, strutting like a true male revue dancer. He pauses twice to do male model poses and expressions. The crowd loves it. Once he reaches the front of the stage, he begins his dance routine, the one I had taught him earlier today. I trained all the men who agreed to take part in this insanity, though a few hours was hardly enough to make them professionals.

We both peek through the curtains.

Reese executes a few dance moves and two pelvic thrusts. Then he moves on to the biggest part of his routine. He grasps the lapels of his costume shirt, and rips them open. He's dressed as a raunchy cowboy, and his outfit is designed to be torn off the way real revue dancers would do. He plucks his cowboy hat off his head and spins it round on one finger while rotating his hips. Finally, he tosses the hat to his wife and rips his trousers off. Now wearing only a G-string, he dances backward and then races forward, diving down to slide forward on his knees. He loses control of that move just a touch, enough that he ends up sideways on the stage and on his back.

Like a true professional, he doesn't let the mishap stop him. He scuttles toward the edge of the stage and lets women stuff Monopoly money inside his waistband. We had all agreed to do that, though it was Reese's idea. Then he leaps to his feet and adds another pelvic thrust for good measure.

The women shriek with delight, particularly Arden.

Reese snatches up his clothes and hat before he jogs off stage.

Hugh rolls his eyes at Reese as the younger bloke slips behind the curtains. "Always a showoff, aren't you?"

"Always." Reese gives Hugh a cheeky grin. "That's why you asked me to be in the naked boy band."

Hugh sighs and switches the microphone on again. "And now, ladies and gents, feast your eyes upon our next dancer. He is such a renowned bit of beefcake that he needs only one name. May I introduce the Titan of the Pitch, the man known worldwide as the Dom—It's Dominic Rigby!"

Screams. Whoops. Clapping.

Dom's old knee injury has been acting up a bit lately, so he doesn't do the full routine. He sticks to moves that don't require him to kneel. No one cares. He strips off his zombie cricketer costume and stands before the horde of salivating females without flinching. He even flexes his biceps and does a few hip pops.

Nick Hunter goes next. His costume is meant to resemble a police uniform, but the shirt has no sleeves. They look as if they've been ripped away. He wears a police-like hat and has a faux badge too, as well as handcuffs.

Hugh introduces him as "Hunk Handsy, the Masseur, also known as Nick Hunter!"

Nick does surprisingly well with his routine, considering that he had been unsure of his ability to dance in the manner required. The crowd loves him, though.

Hugh drops his voice to an even deeper register as he announces the next dancer. "You all know him, and you'd love to have him guard your body." Hugh sucks in a deep breath and shouts, "Please welcome Disco Derek, the New York Adonis—Derek Hahn!"

Derek dresses much like he does when carrying out his bodyguard duties, but he tears the suit off piece by piece, seeming to have a bloody good time firing up the libidos of every woman in the ballroom. Diana, his wife, rushes up to the stage and grasps Derek's tie, the only piece of clothing he still wears, besides his

G-string. She thrusts Monopoly money into his waistband, then grasps his face to kiss him passionately.

He walks off stage with lipstick on his mouth, sauntering like a true exotic dancer.

"And our next hunk of male flesh," Hugh declares, "is someone unexpected. Give an insane round of applause for Monty Cockshire, the Rubdown Artist, known to everyone here as Bennett Montague of Mithoria!"

Ben had asked me for a few tips concerning extra moves he could try, and I gave him several. First, he does a bit of introductory dancing. Ben holds one arm up and the other in front of him, bending his knees as if he's riding a horse, then switches to straightening so he can execute a quick spin followed by some pelvic thrusts. By the time he's done, the crowd is whistling and screaming and generally cheering him on. Ben bows, then trots behind the curtains.

I'm proud of all these blokes. They tried something radically new to them and are succeeding brilliantly.

"Only three more scintillating men for you to devour with your eyes, ladies," Hugh announces. "Are you ready for a bit of Highland heat?"

The women erupt into wild cheering yet again.

"All right, then. Up next, we have a man who loves to feel a vibrating engine between his thighs almost as much as he loves women." Hugh pauses for dramatic effect. "It's Harley Hardtail, the Rider, known to everyone as my best mate, Callum MacTaggart!"

Callum backs up all the way to the wall, then sprints forward only to fall to his knees and slide across the floor. Hugh and I part the curtains for him, and he slides all the way to the edge of the stage. He's dressed as a Highlander, naturally, but with no shirt and his kilt nearly falling off his hips. The plaid is draped over his chest too. He leans back, setting his palms on the floor behind him, and thrusts his hips up in rhythm with the music.

His wife, Kate, barrels her way through the crowd to reach the stage. She flings her arms up and screams, "Harley Hardtail is mine!"

Callum grins and winks. Then he leaps up and does something similar to the electric slide. I wonder if he's having trouble with his knee, like Dom had done. Either way, no one cares. Callum whips off the lower part of his kilt, but leaves the sash hanging over his chest while he pumps his hips a few times, then he gets rid of the sash too. Only his G-string remains.

Harley Hardtail dances his way back through the curtains while making twisting movements with his hands that mimic the way bikers rev their engines. He had chosen his stripper name, Harley Hardtail, because he owns a Harley Davidson motorcycle and "hardtail" is a biker term.

Our emcee is up next. Hugh had tried to convince me to take over while he performs, but I had balked. Since Hugh is very, very good at convincing people to do what he wants, I gave in. Now, it's my turn to drive the crowd wild—not that it takes much with these women.

Hugh smirks and winks at me as he approaches the curtains. "Your turn, mate. Use that voice of yours the way it was meant to be used and make it *sizzle*. Just think of Rachelle in that sexy witch costume. That ought to do the trick."

I do picture Rachelle, and just as Hugh said, it does the trick. I suck in a breath and get started. "Ladies and gents, we have a special treat for you now. He's a rogue, a ladies' man, a rake, and an unrepentant lover of women. You know him. Maybe you even shagged him once or twice."

Hugh throws me a sarcastically disapproving glance.

"Jump into the fires of damnation," I tell the audience, deepening my tone and roughening it up a bit too. "Your soul will be corrupted by the devil himself, if you can survive the heat with Lucifer the Lustful, Lord of the Steam—It's Hugh Parrish!"

Callum pulls the curtain aside, and Hugh dances across the stage, spinning round, sliding sideways, raising his arms above his head to clap and encourage the crowd to do the same. They obey his command. They clap in time with the music, which has a heavy beat beneath the energetic tune. He executes a cowboy hip thrust similar to the one Callum had done, then he performs a cross leg spin before throwing in some pelvic thrusts.

He rips his waistcoat away and tosses it over his shoulder. Then he does a quick moonwalk routine, facing away from the audience, and finally rips his trousers off. They smack into the curtains. He keeps his devil horns, though now he wears only a G-string.

Hugh dances his way back to the curtains and slips between them.

I hand the microphone back to him.

"Ah, yes," Hugh says. "It's time for the headliner. Go for it, mate. These women might eat you alive if you don't get your arse out there immediately."

"Your wife is one of those ravenous women."

"Everyone's wife is. Avery can enjoy looking at nearly naked men all she likes. I do not get jealous."

I approach the curtains, then roll my head and shake out my arms and legs. I'm ready.

"The moment has finally arrived," Hugh purrs into the microphone. "The bloke you've all been waiting to see, the mystery man who inspires fantasies, will be revealed. You know him as the world's most efficient butler. But for one night only, he will perform for you, no holds barred. They call him Rod Thruster, Maverick of the Wild West End, King of the Pelvic Thrusts—Show your love for Kendall!"

I saunter out onto the stage and stop. Hugh and I had discussed this moment, and he will keep the intro music on repeat until I've done what I need to do.

Rachelle sits at the table closest to the stage. When she gazes up at me with love and lust in her eyes, I know she wants me to do this. So, I saunter up to the edge of the stage, kneel, and offer her my hands. "Come up here, darling. You are my inspiration for this routine."

She grasps my hands, letting me hoist her onto the stage. Callum has just placed a chair in the center of the performance area, facing the audience, and now vanishes behind the curtain again.

"Rod Thruster has chosen his ingénue," Hugh announces. "Are you ready to be seduced, Rachelle?"

She sits down on the chair and throws her arms up. "Hell, yeah, I'm ready! Bring it on, Lucifer."

My gladiator costume doesn't give me much to strip away, but that doesn't matter. As the intro music grows louder and faster, I hook a finger under her chin and rub my thumb over her bottom lip.

"It's time to show you who I am, darling. Right now."

Chapter Twenty-One

Rachelle

Kendall backs away from me and halts, waiting a few agonizing seconds while the women in the audience begin to clap in time with the music. Then the song shifts into a faster rhythm as an electric guitar plays decadent chords. I can't take my gaze off Kendall. He seems more confident and determined than ever before, not to mention hot as hell.

He dances toward me, making slithery arm movements, and sinuously writhes just enough to make the moves even hotter.

I'm getting warmer every second.

Then he dances around my chair, performing slight variations on the moves he's already done. When he stops in front of me, I find myself staring at his groin. But when he starts rolling his entire body, starting with his torso and arms, then adding his hips and legs, I have trouble pulling in a full breath. His moves are serpentine in the sexiest way, and they highlight all his muscles.

He drops to the floor and slaps a hand on the surface. Then he spreads his thighs only to slide them together again, repeating the move over and over at a rapid pace.

The screaming from the other women in this ballroom has grown even louder than ever.

Kendall lies down on his belly and crawls toward me with his legs bent and his arms straight, moving in that same super-sexy, fluid motion. Watching him inch toward me that way, I get so wet and achy that my pulse revs into overdrive. I need a fan. Somebody bring me a damn fan. I can't even yell at someone to do that because Kendall has left me speechless. So, I wave my own hand in my face, though it doesn't help.

But when he reaches me, with his head near my feet, and gazes up at me with sheer lust in his eyes...

My chest is heaving. My heart is pounding. I bite my lip because it's all I can do. Oh yeah, I am Rod Thruster's biggest fan.

Then he crawls away from me in the same slow, serpentine way.

Kendall winks at me.

I pretend to faint, and the crowd screams even more.

Rod Thruster leaps to his feet, legs spread. He leans sideways while sliding his palms down his chest, straight to his groin. The leather flaps of his costume move with him as he cups his dick.

Then he pumps his hips four times, pulling his elbows back at the same time.

And he runs toward me, falling to his knees to glide across the floor, only to skid to a halt inches away from me and spring to his feet. "Time to return to your table, darling. The big finale is coming."

I might come too if he doesn't stop looking so lickably delicious and thoroughly edible.

Kendall picks me up, sauntering to the edge of the stage, and sets me down at my table. He smirks and winks, then walks away. Now positioned a few yards from the edge of the platform, he stands perfectly still yet relaxed.

What, he isn't going to strip? That was the whole point of this show.

The curtains flutter, and Kendall's crew takes the stage behind him. All of them wear only their G-strings—except for Kendall. Hugh isn't on stage yet. But then I hear him doing his emcee thing again.

"And now, ladies and gents, for the climax of our hedonistic show, we will all dance for you. The showstopping finale begins now!"

Hugh emerges to take his place with the other men.

Kendall, standing at the front, simply taps one foot to the pounding, suggestive music as his fellow dancers perform a synchronized routine that highlights all the moves they had employed earlier.

But Kendall still only stands there tapping his foot.

His gaze flicks to me, and he winks yet again.

The music throbs harder, the tempo quickening gradually.

Suddenly, Kendall begins to dance. At first, he does the same moves as the other men. But after a moment, he switches to doing his own routine that meshes with their moves but proves he is the king of the pelvic thrusts for sure. He executes all kinds of quick, hot moves—like that body roll thing and light-footed dancing similar to what Gene Kelly might have done back in the day. But Gene Kelly never got filthy. Kendall does, and I love it.

As the music reaches a crescendo, I know the performance is about to end.

Kendall drops to the floor on his back, writhing in that erotic, smooth, and mind-blowing way. Then he rises to his knees just as smoothly. He peels the chest strap away, tossing it aside. One by one, he peels the arm straps away too, all while thrusting his hips and performing light-footed dance moves.

He rips the gladiator kilt off now, flinging it toward...me.

I catch it and whoop.

The only clothing on his body is those boots and a G-string.

Kendall leaps to his feet and cups his groin, then raises his arms while thrusting his hips. Just as the last note of the music echoes in the ballroom, he spins around and flings an object over his shoulder. It lands on my lap.

It's his G-string.

Kendall spins around once before sauntering behind the curtains with his fellow dancers right behind him.

Did he just—I mean, no, he wouldn't—But I'm holding his G-string in my hand, so yeah. Kendall just stripped buck naked.

I sit here in my chair just staring at the empty stage. The spotlight has been shut off, but the smaller lights around the edges of the platform still burn.

Avery gives my arm a shake. "Rachelle, are you okay? You look kind of stunned. I can't imagine you're shocked into paralysis because Kendall went for the full monty."

"What?" I blink rapidly several times, then turn my head toward Avery. "No, I'm not shocked to see a naked man. But I never thought Kendall would go all the way like that. He's incredible—as a dancer, as a boyfriend, and as a man—but he's been ashamed for years because of his old job. Seeing him ditch all his clothes in front of everyone left me speechless because he finally let go of those old fears."

"And you had something to do with that too."

The curtains fly open, and Kendall stalks across the stage wearing his G-string again. No one here is shocked, except for me. He hops off the stage, landing right in front of me.

"Kendall? What are you doing?"

He scoops me up in his arms and marches across the whole ballroom, veering out into the hallway and heading straight for the stairs that lead to the second floor. Lots of noise erupts in our wake, but Kendall doesn't even flinch. He keeps going until we reach our bedroom suite. Then he kicks the door shut behind us and drops me onto the bed.

"Strip, Rachelle, now."

The only light in the room emanates from the moonglow coming in through the windows. I push up onto my elbows and study his nude form, glistening with sweat.

"What are you doing, Kendall?"

He fists his hands, then loosens them. "I need to fuck you right now."

I push up into a sitting position. "You could at least try a little seduction first."

He rolls his head side to side as if he's ironing out kinks in his neck. "Please, darling, I'm so randy I almost can't stand it. Watching you watch me was the most erotic experience I've ever had, particularly when you were sitting on the stage with me."

Yeah, the bulge in his G-string has gotten bigger since he brought me upstairs. And I'm just as horny as he is. Why am I acting like I don't want him to screw me? I think my raging hormones are messing with my head. I can't think straight, especially with him standing there looking so edible. I want to nibble on him from head to toe and then do it all over again.

"Sit down on the bed, Kendall, please. Keep your feet on the floor."

He tilts his head to one side. "What are you thinking of, pet?"

"I want to eat you up. Then I want you to do the same to me."

"We could do that simultaneously."

"Let's do it my way. I've wanted to taste you since the day we met, but I haven't gotten around to that until tonight."

He ambles over to me and sits on the bed's edge. "What now?"

"Just relax and let me do all the work."

Kendall spreads his legs and leans back, setting his hands on the mattress behind his ass. "Go on, I'm ready."

I hop off the bed and remove my clothes, then kneel between his legs. The length of his erection waves in front of me. The tip is red and glistening with moisture. I lay my arms on his thighs as I lean forward and drag my tongue over the crown of his cock.

He jerks and gasps.

I do that again, only this time I curl my tongue to taste the underside of his crown. The salty flavor makes me moan with a hunger I can't disguise. Can't believe how much I want to do this for him, but we've had an intense lust for each other since the day we met. It's chemistry, the kind that could burn down Sommerleigh House.

Kendall releases the longest, most satisfied sigh I've ever heard as I take his length into my mouth and coil my tongue around it over and over again. That salty flavor infiltrates my mouth even more now. I moan and massage his inner thighs while I work his cock, pumping with my mouth, getting so into it that with every stroke I take him as far inside my mouth as I possibly can.

He begins a rhythm of sucking in a breath and blowing it out, groaning with every exhalation. I slide a hand up to his balls and massage his sac until he's breathing hard, his chest heaving.

"Bloody hell, love. You're driving me mad."

The rough tone of his voice pushes me to increase the pace. I need to swallow everything he can give me. A shiver of delight rushes through me at that realization. But as much as I want that, I need to draw out his pleasure for as long as possible.

I pull my mouth away, licking my lips with languorous strokes of my tongue. "Oh, God, Kendall. I want to devour every inch of you."

"Bugger me, I can't—" He gasps when I dive my head down to curl my tongue inside his navel. "I can't stand this torture for much longer. I love it, but it's…so intense."

"If you tell me to stop, I will. I'll suck you off right now."

He gazes down at me, his cheeks pink and his chest rising and falling heavily. "Don't stop yet."

"Mm, I'm glad you said that. I've got an idea." I sit back on my heels. "Turn around the other way."

His brows pinch together. "What? I don't understand."

"I want you to kneel on the floor, up against the bed, and lay your arms on the mattress in front of you. Got it?"

"All right," he says slowly.

"Before we do anything else, I need to make sure you really want to do this. I don't want to push you into anything that makes you uncomfortable."

He chuckles, though it's a touch breathless. "I stripped naked and performed a raunchy dance in front of all our mates. This won't make me uneasy. It's just that I'm not sure what you're about."

"Do you trust me?"

"Completely."

I pat his knee. "Then do what I said."

While I waddle backward, he slides off the bed to kneel on the floor. He rotates away from me, placing his arms on the mattress. "I'm ready, Rachelle. Is this the correct position?"

"Yep, that looks good." I examine his position and realize I need to tweak it a touch. "Actually, why don't you shimmy backward a little. I need some space between your body and the bed."

He crawls backward on his knees until his elbows are resting on the very edge of the bed and his body is angled away from it.

"That's perfect, Kendall."

I move around beside him so I can sidle between him and the bed. His cock is plastered to my cheek. I sink down on my heels, giving myself a better position, with his dick directly in front of my mouth. "Hold on, baby. I'm about to blow your mind."

"Of that I have no doubts."

This time when I take him into my mouth, I can do much more than just suck on his delicious dick. As much as I hunger for a Kendall lollipop, I love having the chance to tease him this way with one of my hands while I wrap the other around the base of his cock and start pumping from both ends—the base of his erection with my hand, and the rest of it with my mouth.

I slide me free hand between his legs to slip one finger between his ass cheeks, just barely teasing him with the tip of that finger.

He gasps.

"Is this okay, Kendall?"

"Yes. It felt…rather good."

"Oh, I can do better than 'rather good.' Just wait." I tickle his anus with that finger, making him gasp again. "Still okay?"

"Yes, love, keep going."

I gently slide that finger into his hole while I resume sucking on his dick. He groans, and I know that means he's enjoying this. I'm about to try something I've never done before, so I'm sure he's never done it either. But somehow I know he'll love it.

Since I've got hold of his dick, I use one finger to tease his balls. That makes him jerk. While I start working his cock more vigorously, making little grunting sounds of my own, I begin to gently fuck him with my other finger.

"Bugger me, Rachelle, this is—Ah, it's incredible."

I use another finger on the same hand to pet the outside of his anus, even while I keep fucking him that way. His breathing has grown harsher and faster, and I can hear the sound of his fingernails rasping on the sheets. His body goes rigid. He seems to stop breathing.

And suddenly, he comes.

The jet of his release spills onto my tongue and spreads the delicious flavor of him. He can't stop himself from thrusting into my mouth to release even more. He reaches down to clasp my breast, mercilessly flicking his thumb over the peak of my nipple. That sensation does something to me that I've never felt before.

It makes me come. My body tenses, and then the spasms inside me hit, the waves undulating inside me. This feels different from a regular orgasm. The spasms are deeper and rounder somehow.

After two more thrusts, he's done.

But he keeps on flicking his thumb while I cry out and the climax rolls on and on. When it finally ends, I crawl out from under him and sag against the bed.

"Wow, Kendall. We are amazing at sex."

"Yes, darling, we are."

Chapter Twenty-Two

Kendall

I wake up after the best night's sleep of my life to find that I had not dreamed that last night happened. The sun shines in through the windows just like it had done the day before, and Rachelle is cuddled against me as she has done every night since we renewed our acquaintance. I could easily believe that Halloween night had been a wonderful, bizarre, risqué dream. Yet I know it happened. I returned to my roots and became Rod Thruster again, for a one-night-only performance.

And I don't regret even one moment of it.

While Rachelle remains asleep, I simply lie here enjoying the sweet silence and the comfort of having the woman I love in my arms.

Until a fist bangs on the door. "Wakey-wakey, Kendall and Rachelle."

I groan and make a rude face, though the man who has annoyed me can't see that. "Piss off, Hugh."

"My wife won't be happy if you aren't there for breakfast. We've let you both sleep late, but it's time to rise and shine. If you sleep any longer, you'll be eating lunch instead of breakfast."

Is it really that late? I carefully stretch one arm out to turn the bedside clock just enough that I can see the hands on its face. "Blimey. Rachelle, wake up. It's nearly ten o'clock in the morning."

"Are you coming?" Hugh asks. "You may interpret that any way you like."

That cheeky sod.

"You have nineteen minutes, Kendall. Rouse Rachelle and get dressed." He pauses, then adds in an even cheekier tone, "You might just have time to give her an encore performance."

"Sod off, Lord Sommerleigh."

He chuckles, then whistles as he walks away.

Rachelle moans and wriggles, though her eyes remain closed. "Was that Hugh?"

"Yes, love, it was." I pat her arse. "Wake up, darling. We've slept late, and it's time for breakfast."

She moans again as she stretches her entire body and yawns. Then, at last, she opens her eyes and smiles. "I love waking up this way, with you naked and tousled, waiting to ravish me."

"Afraid we don't have time for that. Get dressed, or Hugh might kick the door open and drag us down to the dining room in the nude."

Her sleepy, sexy smile gives me a pang in my chest. "After last night, I have a whole new view of nudity."

"You seemed to enjoy the show."

"I enjoyed watching the other guys." She pushes herself up on one elbow and leans toward me. "But I loved your routine so much that I almost came just watching you."

For a moment, I can't convince my vocal cords to function. Then an emotion surges up inside me, so strong that I can't hold back. "I love you, Rachelle, and I want to spend the rest of my life with you."

She freezes.

Bollocks. I've said too much too soon, haven't I?

Then Rachelle smiles and kisses me. "I love you too, Kendall. Never felt this way before, but I won't second guess my feelings, not anymore. I want to be with you for the rest of my life too."

My lips have stretched into what I suddenly realize is a joyous grin. Yes, I've found the right woman at last. But I have one more confession. "It's time I told you my full name."

She sits up and rubs her hands together. "Ooh, this is exciting."

"No, it actually isn't." I take a breath and do it. "My name is Jolyon Kendall Halfenaked."

Rachelle stares at me for a moment, then bursts out laughing. "That's your big secret? Sure, Halfenaked is a weird name. But I was expecting something way more bizarre."

"Jolyon is rather unusual too. I prefer Kendall."

"So do I. Your middle and last names both suit you. Kind of weird that a man called Halfenaked wound up becoming a stripper."

"I agree. Perhaps it was fate. I never believed in that until I met you."

Once we're dressed, we jog down the stairs into the foyer and bump into Dominic and Chelsea, who are also heading for the dining room. They seem rather excited, but when I ask them why, they won't tell me.

"Just go into the dining room," Dom says. "You'll see."

Hand in hand, Rachelle and I enter the room. I halt just past the threshold, suddenly incapable of moving even one more inch.

Rachelle glances at me worriedly. "Kendall, what's wrong?"

"Nothing." I release her hand, shuffling forward three paces, and gawp at the couple in front of me. "Mum? Dad? What are you doing here?"

He surges toward me, grasping my shoulders briefly before he hauls me into a boisterous hug. Dad thumps my back several times, and when he finally pulls away, I swear his eyes are glistening with the start of tears. "Kenny, I'm so sorry for the way we behaved all those years ago. But Mum and I have always been proud of you."

I still can do nothing but gawp at him.

My father hugs me again. "Rosalyn and Hugh told us all about what happened after you left London. They knew you were humiliated by everyone finding out about your job at that club." He turns toward Mum and clasps her hand, drawing her closer to us. "We should have been more supportive of you. All your mates made fun of you, and all my coworkers harassed me. But I should never have let what other people think affect our family. I'm sorry, Kenny."

Mum rushes at me, pulling me into a hug while tears trickle down her cheeks. "I'm so sorry, pet. We both are, and we're so proud of you. We should have told you that ages ago."

Dominic and Chelsea move out of the way to allow someone else to approach. Two someones, actually.

My brother gives me a quick hug and slaps my arm. "Glad I wasn't here last night to see you reprise your old gig. No offense, Kenny, but I don't need to see your naked arse."

"Neither do I," my sister says. "Once was more than enough."

Rachelle has been standing beside me this whole time, and I know now is the moment to share my latest news. "Mum, Dad, I'd like to introduce you to the woman I plan to marry, Rachelle Buckholtz. And Rachelle, these are my parents, Martin and Marjorie Halfenaked. And the annoying arse beside me is my brother, Spencer Halfenaked. Beside him is my lovely sister Belinda Gibson, though we call her Bindy."

Mum slaps my brother's arm. "Belinda got married and gave us two wonderful grandchildren. Now Kendall has a girl, and they'll have babies soon. But when will you settle down, Spencer?"

He makes a pained face. "Could we not discuss this now?"

Lord Sommerleigh rings a bell, silencing our discussion. "Why don't we enjoy our breakfast? You can harass your children later, Mrs. Halfenaked." Hugh can't fully suppress his smirk. "I think I prefer to keep calling you Kendall, mate."

"Yes, I prefer that too."

"We have another surprise, but it won't arrive until this afternoon." Hugh helps his wife get seated, then sits down at the head of the table. "Mildred has created a true feast for all of us. Please take a seat and enjoy it."

Breakfast turns into a boisterous event with everyone laughing and telling tales about the wild things they and their mates have done. My parents don't care to hear the details about last night's big bash, but they love to hear about how I met Rachelle. I leave out the naughty bits. And after the meal, Rachelle and I take my family out onto the patio to discuss things in private.

"We were never ashamed of you, Kenny," Mum says. "But we didn't deal with the scandal very well. We thought by never talking about it again, you would feel more comfortable coming to visit us."

"Seems like we had it the wrong way round," Dad admits. "We should've talked about it, so you'd know it doesn't bother us anymore. Hasn't done for a long time. We're more sorry than you could know that we gave you the impression we're ashamed of you."

"No worries," I tell him. "That's all in the past, and it's partly my fault that we don't see each other often enough. I thought you and Mum would feel uncomfortable if I invited you to Sommerleigh."

"Rosalyn is a great lady. Can't picture her turning away working-class folk like us."

"No, she would never do that."

I've had so many things wrong, but all of that is in the past now. My family and the Parrishes get on smashingly. Dad even hugs Hugh when I tell him that Lord Sommerleigh has become like a brother to me. Mum hugs him and kisses his cheek. Hugh seems amused by their behavior.

In the afternoon, we all gather on the lawn for a casual round of cricket. My father joins in the game, though I had no idea he had ever played cricket before.

"When I was a schoolboy," he tells me, "I joined the team so I could get out of maths class twice a week. When I was sixteen, I'd figured out that girls loved a man in cricket kit." He winks at Mum. "That's how I met your mother. She was my best groupie."

Mum rests her head on his shoulder. "You were so sexy back then, Martin. We all wanted to be your girlfriend. But I'm the one who married you."

After the cricket match, Rachelle and Spencer strike up a conversation. She's been curious about my brother ever since she first met him. "Spencer, are you married like Bindy?"

"No. I'm too busy to date."

"But now that Kendall is in a relationship, don't you want to find a girlfriend?"

"Maybe later. I'm younger than Kenny, so I have plenty of time to worry about starting a family. Or maybe I never will do that."

Marjorie smacks her son's arm with the back of her hand. "Spencer, you must give us babies. Can't let Bindy and Kendall do all the work."

I snap upright on the chaise I'd been relaxing on. "Me? Rachelle and I aren't even engaged yet. Please don't start pressuring us to give you grandchildren. Let Bindy's lot fulfill your baby dreams for now."

Spencer nods decisively. "I second that, Kenny."

"How many times have I told you that I prefer to be called Kendall?"

"Oh, somewhere near a thousand. At least Dad stopped calling you Jolly."

"Only because I mounted a campaign to eradicate that nickname."

My father laughs. "I remember that. You refused to clean up your room until we all started calling you Kendall. You were so bloody determined that we decided it was easier to just give in. Besides, your room was starting to smell."

Yes, I'm chuffed that my family are all here.

But Rachelle gets a surprise too when her parents arrive.

Paulette Gérard and Rusty Buckholtz aren't quite what I expected. I suppose I assumed Rachelle's mother would be haughty, since she walked away from her daughter. But she's actually quite normal and lovely to chat with. Rusty is too.

Just a few months ago, I'd been content to perform my butler duties and nothing else. Now, my entire life has been upended, and I love it.

Epilogue

Rachelle
Two Months Later

I sit on a chaise on the lawn at Sommerleigh, soaking up the sun and marveling at how much my life has changed.

Six months ago, I was lonely, and I'd given up on finding the right man—or any man. My dreams of getting married and having kids had evaporated. Then I bumped into Kendall and promptly ran away from him. Four months later, I hunted him down. That was the defining moment, when everything changed. Though I couldn't have guessed it at the time, I had met my soul mate.

Now, we have the perfect life together. We aren't married yet, but we do share the big suite that we'd slept in during that wild Halloween weekend. Hugh and Avery insisted that, since we're a couple, Kendall should have a real suite, rather than just the bachelor pad where he'd been living for seventeen years.

Yeah, it was time for him to level up.

The sun feels so good on my face. Okay, yeah, it's now New Year's Day, and the weather isn't perfect. But I've bundled up with a warm wool coat that Kendall insisted I should borrow from him if I'm going to sit outside. The weather isn't as cold as he tried to tell me it was. The sun makes all the difference, though.

The world's hottest butler emerges from the solarium and marches across the patio, down the steps, to halt beside me. "Are you pretending not to be cold? Or are you legitimately not cold?"

"It's legit." I pat the chaise next to mine. "Sit down, Kendall. It's Saturday, and even you take the weekend off."

"Yes. But I was waylaid by Spencer, who has been playing Scrabble with Bindy, Avery, and Hugh. They needed me to break a tie in their game. They'd been arguing about whether some word or other was spelled correctly." Kendall drops onto the chaise and stretches his legs out. "I told them to piss off and figure it out on their own."

The sound of children giggling echoes across the lawn from somewhere on the other side of the house. That would be Rosalyn, my parents, and Kendall's parents having fun with the kids. Bindy and her husband, Charles, wanted to stay inside and play games with Spencer and Hugh. Since I saw Hugh and Avery wandering into the garden a little while ago, they have clearly left the game room, aka the sitting room.

Kendall stretches his arm out, offering me his hand.

I lay my palm on his, and we both smile at the same time. "Life is good, isn't it?"

"Our life is bloody fantastic, I'd say."

"You're right. It is amazing."

He gazes at me steadily for a moment, which usually means he has something serious to tell me. He was happy thirty seconds ago.

"What's wrong?" I ask. "You look tense all of a sudden."

"Everything is perfect. Or rather, it will be perfect in a moment." He slides off his chaise and kneels beside me. Then he clasps my left hand. "I can't imagine my life without you anymore, and that means I need to do everything possible to keep you with me. To that end…"

I can guess what he wants to say, and my heart speeds up.

He reaches into his pocket with his free hand, pulling out a small satin box. As he flips the lid up, he smiles with a depth of love I've never seen before. "Rachelle Marie Buckholtz, will you marry me?"

I shriek. Then I spring forward and throw my arms around his neck. "Yes, Kendall, of course I want to marry you."

"Wouldn't you like to have the ring, pet?"

"Oh. Yeah. Right." I can't help giggling a little bit. I'm genuinely giddy right now. Kendall raises the ring to my finger and slips it on. And I giggle again. "It fits perfectly."

I throw my arms around him one more time, peppering kisses all over his face.

Someone starts clapping.

Not me. Not Kendall.

Another someone whistles.

Kendall pulls away and shields his gaze with one hand while squinting at the two people heading toward us. "Is that your mother? And your father?"

"Yes, it is." I jump up and wave to them. "Come over here! We've got big news."

Kendall rises and comes up beside me, folding his hand around mine.

Mom and Dad finally reach us, both smiling broadly. Mom clasps my face and kisses both my cheeks. "*Ma chérie*, this is wonderful news. Kendall is a wonderful man, and you are such a beautiful couple."

"How did you know we got engaged?"

Dad chuckles. "Sommerleigh House has an echo problem. When you shrieked, I think they could hear you in London."

Mom grabs Kendall's face now and firmly kisses both his cheeks. "Kendall, *mon beau*, I know you will take care of Rachelle and love her as she deserves to be loved."

"You have my word, I will." Kendall lifts my hand and kisses the diamond ring. "Rachelle is the other half of my soul."

Dad rushes into the house to get Kendall's parents and his siblings. They're just as happy as we are when we share the news.

Martin and Marjorie get here first and smother their oldest son with joyful babbling that none of us understand because they're crying too. We know they're thrilled. That's all that matters.

Then Kendall's brother and sister race up to us.

"This is wonderful!" Bindy says while grinning. "I've always wanted a sister, and now I have one."

Spencer gives me a quick, firm hug. "This is smashing news. I've never seen my brother as happy as he's been since you two got together, Rachelle. But, Kendall, who will be your best man at the wedding?"

"Well, ah…"

"Relax. I assume Hugh will be the best man, and I'm not offended by that."

"Let's discuss that when the time comes."

At brunch, we share our news with everyone else. Hugh jumps out of his chair and ruffles Kendall's hair, then hugs him while he's still sitting down.

"It's brilliant!" Hugh shouts. "Bloody fucking brilliant!"

When Hugh sits down again, grinning like a happy fool, Kendall turns his attention to his brother. "So, Spencer, have you heard about the American Wives Club?"

"Oh, no. I will not be dragged into that rubbish. Dominic told me all about it."

"Then you know it's a wonderful thing. The club has changed the lives of dozens of couples."

"Not getting married, Hugh. My career is my mistress."

Kendall shakes his head at his brother. "That's what I thought too. But you'll see, Spence. One barmy woman changed my life, and it's all thanks to the American Wives Club."

He's right about that. Those women fight for love like warriors fight to win battles.

Once the excitement dies down and brunch is over, I finally have a moment to let everything sink in. I'm getting married. My insane plot to hunt down Kendall turned out to be the best risk I'd ever taken. I wouldn't change a minute of the past six months.

And I can't wait for our future to unfold.

Want more of Spencer Halfenaked? Experience his story in *One Hot Moment*.

Love the *Hot Brits* series?

Visit AnnaDurand.com

to subscribe to her newsletter for updates on forthcoming books in this series plus exclusive content!

Anna Durand is a bestselling, multi-award-winning author of contemporary and paranormal romance. Her books have earned bestseller status on every major retailer and wonderful reviews from readers around the world. But that's the boring spiel. Here are the really cool things you want to know about Anna!

Born on Lackland Air Force Base in Texas, Anna grew up moving here, there, and everywhere thanks to her dad's job as an instructor pilot. She's lived in Texas (twice), Mississippi, California (twice), Michigan (twice), and Alaska—and now Ohio.

As for her writing, Anna has always made up stories in her head, but she didn't write them down until her teen years. Those first awful books went into the trash can a few years later, though she learned a lot from those stories. Eventually, she would pen her first romance novel, the paranormal romance *Willpower*, and she's never looked back since.

Want even more details about Anna? Get access to her extended bio when you subscribe to her newsletter and download the free bonus ebook, *Hot Scots Confidential*. You'll also get hot deleted scenes, character interviews, fun facts, and more! Plus you'll receive the short story *Tempted by a Kiss* and mutliple bonus chapters in both ebook and audiobook formats.

Visit AnnaDurand.com to sign up.

www.ingramcontent.com/pod-product-compliance
Lightning Source LLC
LaVergne TN
LVHW011939070526
838202LV00054B/4724